There was nothing for it. Clairey couldn't deny how much she'd enjoyed herself today.

Spending the day with Drexel and Marnie had been some of the most enjoyable hours she could remember in a long while. In fact, she couldn't recall a time she'd so thoroughly felt joy. Certainly not after she'd been so unceremoniously forced out of her home by her mother. Not that the days she'd lived in that house before her banishment could be described as anything resembling happy.

On top of it all, Drexel had needed her today. He and Marnie both had.

It was a heady feeling and she knew she had to tread carefully. No one had actually needed her before. Not really.

How in the world could she turn her back on that? She couldn't.

She turned in her seat to tell him before she could change her mind. "I'll do it," she blurted out without giving herself a chance to think any more on it. "I'll take your offer to be your nanny for Marnie."

Dear Reader,

I'm so pleased you're about to meet Drexel and Clairey. Their story is a dear one to my heart. In it, I try to explore what it means to feel a sense of belonging, whether that might be within one's birth family or a found family.

In Clairey's case, her place within the world was shattered early in her life due to a tremendous loss. Drexel never seemed to fit in with the family he was born into.

They both wonder if they'll ever feel a true sense of belonging.

One little girl is the trigger that leads them both to discovering the answer to that question. Along the way, they also find love.

I hope you enjoy their journey.

Nina

Whisked into the Billionaire's World

—

Nina Singh

ISBN-13: 978-1-335-40712-2

Whisked into the Billionaire's World

Harlequin Enterprises ULC
22 Adelaide St. West, 41st Floor
Toronto, Ontario M5H 4E3, Canada
www.Harlequin.com

Printed in U.S.A.

Nina Singh lives just outside Boston, Massachusetts, with her husband, children and a very rambunctious Yorkie. After several years in the corporate world, she finally followed the advice of family and friends to "give the writing a go, already." She's oh-so-happy she did. When not at her keyboard, she likes to spend time on the tennis court or golf course. Or immersed in a good read.

Books by Nina Singh

Harlequin Romance

How to Make a Wedding

From Tropical Fling to Forever

Destination Brides

Swept Away by the Venetian Millionaire

Reunited with Her Italian Billionaire
Tempted by Her Island Millionaire
Christmas with Her Secret Prince
Captivated by the Millionaire
Their Festive Island Escape
Her Billionaire Protector
Spanish Tycoon's Convenient Bride
Her Inconvenient Christmas Reunion
From Wedding Fling to Baby Surprise
Around the World with the Millionaire

Visit the Author Profile page at Harlequin.com.

To all those still trying to find where they fit in best.

CHAPTER ONE

SHE JUST COULDN'T do it. She couldn't allow this couple to tie the knot.

Clairey Robi knew she would lose her job for what she was about to do. But the two people in question had no business getting married. The results would be too toxic.

And there was a child involved.

She'd been on the fence until she thought about the child. Given what Clairey had herself dealt with growing up, how could she risk what might happen to the little girl? Still, what she was about to do was rather daunting. And she was just starting to like this job. Plus, she needed it badly. Really badly. Clairey was at the level of broke where she was actually being charged for it. The bank kept imposing fees on her measly account for insufficient funds. What a racket that was.

Determined, she brushed all those annoying thoughts aside and continued across the resort lobby, aware that the havoc that she was about to cause was sure to wreak havoc in her own life for years to come.

The sound of sharp, pointed heels sounded behind her. Tessa Gilman was striding next to her a moment later.

"You still determined to go through with this?" the other woman asked. They'd discussed Clairey's quandary at breakfast in the resort's outdoor café by the pool area.

"I wouldn't be able to live with myself if I didn't." That was the absolute truth. How different might her own life have been if someone had ever bothered to step up for her? If there'd been someone who'd cared enough?

But there hadn't been.

She couldn't just stand by and watch another child potentially go through what she herself had.

Tess frowned but Clairey didn't slow her steps. If she hesitated now, she might not go through with it at all. "I hope you know what you're doing." Tessa elongated the final word into three syllables.

"Of course I don't. I tossed and turned all night with the decision. Agonized over it." That was no exaggeration. Clairey's eyes stung, red from her restless night.

"Okay," Tessa answered. "As long as you're prepared for Louis's reaction. He's going to be livid."

Clairey cringed at the mention of her boss's name. The man was a grump in a sales-rack suit on the best of days.

"I know," Clairey answered, but she kept walking at her steady rate toward the secondary conference room.

Tessa for some reason felt the need to drive home her very obvious point and kept talking. "He is absolutely going to fire you. And it's not like he'll give you any kind of recommendation to help you get another job."

Clairey sighed. Why was Tessa repeating all this? They'd gotten into all of the unpleasant outcomes this morning at breakfast. The fact that she'd be out of a job with no real prospects of finding another one anytime soon was one of the major reasons for her hours-long insomnia last night.

"Why do you feel so strongly about this?" she asked.

The question gave Clairey pause. Tessa knew why. Maybe not the full story but enough of the overall gist.

Clairey had no interest in dredging up the devastating memories. Especially not now with what she was about to do.

To make matters worse, the timing was just so off: just when she thought she might be able to save enough money to be able to stop crashing on Tessa's couch and find a place of her own. That clearly wouldn't be happening any-time soon. Not with all the student loans she had to pay off.

Best to just get this over with. She made it to the double doors of the meeting room by the concierge desk and pulled them wide open, then stepped inside with a deep, fortifying breath. Seven pairs of curious eyes immediately whipped in her direction.

Okay. Maybe the entrance had been a bit dramatic. But even a moment's hesitation might have caused her to delay or perhaps even change her mind altogether.

She turned to Tessa for some support and courage but only saw her friend's back as the other woman made a hasty retreat down the wide corridor back toward the main lobby.

So much for friendly support. With another deep breath, Clairey stepped into the room and pulled the doors shut behind her.

The seven in attendance sat around a conference table, various binders and loose papers strewn about its surface. Seven? Why was there someone else among the group? The bride, her mother, the groom, the photographer, the florist and their wedding planner. As for the other gentleman, Clairey couldn't guess who he was. She'd never seen him before.

Clairey's gaze fell to the one unexpected attendee. And she had trouble regaining her focus.

The man was almost unnaturally handsome. Jet-black wavy hair that framed a face of tanned olive skin, his eyes the color of warm amber. His suit jacket hung over the back of his chair.

And he was staring right at her with intense scrutiny.

Who in the world was he? She'd thought she'd met every member of the wedding party. And she absolutely would have remembered meeting this man.

"Clairey?" Emma, the bride's mother finally addressed her. "I'm sorry. I didn't realize we were expecting you for this meeting."

Clairey managed to somehow tear her face away from Mr. Tall Dark and Handsome. Not that it was easy.

"I'm not here for the meeting," she finally answered once she'd found her voice.

"Then, why are you here?" Danielle, the bride, asked.

Here it was. The moment of no return. "To tell you that I strongly believe tomorrow shouldn't happen."

The woman certainly knew how to make an entrance. Drexel Osoman stilled in the act of signing his name to yet another check, made out to the florist this time, and studied the meeting-crasher.

She looked more than ready for a fight.

And what she'd just said certainly qualified as fighting words. Had she really just declared that tomorrow's wedding should not go forward? His soon-to-be sister-in-law scowled across the table. "I'm sorry. Is this some kind of joke?"

Drex realized just how anxious the young woman was. *Clairey* the bride's mother had called her. She was shaking visibly, her fists clenched tight at her sides. Her eyes were wide with apprehension.

Yet, she was clearly still determined to go through with what she'd come in here to do.

Drex couldn't help but be impressed.

She shook her head now with a brisk movement that sent her wavy chestnut curls bouncing. "No. It's no joke. I've come here to say I strongly object to the two of you getting married."

An audible and collective gasp echoed throughout the room. Her eyes seemed to have landed on him as she finished her sentence. As if looking for some confirmation or support from his direction. As much as Drex agreed with her, it wasn't as if he could actually say so.

She continued. "I think doing so would be a terrible mistake that would only lead to unnecessary suffering."

Wow. That was rather direct. Another round of gasps followed her words.

Drex took a moment to study her. She was...

striking. It was the first word that came to mind. Her long dark hair cascaded down her elegant shoulders. Grayish-blue eyes outlined in dark charcoal. Smooth, tanned skin. She looked like she could be an extra in one of those old Hollywood films about Cleopatra.

No. Strike that. This woman was no extra. She would definitely be the lead. He gave a shake of his head. What was wrong with him? He had more pressing matters at the moment than this woman's notable looks.

Drex leaned back in his chair and scanned the others in the room. One by one, they all seemed to turn in his direction with clear expectation.

How and why had he become the decider on exactly what to do about the current scenario? He'd only arrived at the crack of dawn this morning, for heaven's sake.

The meeting with his overseas partner-to-be had not gone well. The man was culturally traditional and didn't want to budge on any of the more modern ideas for the project. It had taken all of Drex's wits and willpower to maintain a steady resolve with the negotiations. All he wanted now was a long shower and a chance to catch up on some of his other demands. He really was in no mood for any of this.

But seeing as he'd found himself in the middle of some kind of strange standoff with no real resolution in sight, it was clear he was going to have to take the lead here. Putting his pen down with a resigned sigh, Drex cleared his throat.

"I've just arrived, Miss…?"

"Robi. My name is Clairey Robi," she supplied.

"Ms. Robi. I'm Drexel Osoman. The groom's older brother."

She made some sort of small movement with her shoulders, not quite a shrug.

Drex continued. "I was due here earlier but have been busy with a rather complex business deal and couldn't get here until near dawn this morning." If the irritation he felt was evident in his voice, there was nothing for it. He didn't need all this drama on top of everything else happening in his life at the moment. "May I ask, what exactly is the issue here?"

She sucked in a breath. "It's like I said earlier, Mr. Osoman."

"Call me Drexel, please. Or Drex."

She visibly swallowed. "It's like I said earlier," she repeated. "I strongly object to the marriage moving forward. I know I'm merely a stranger here—"

Drexel cut her off once more. "Indeed, you are."

She flinched ever so slightly. "I'm aware. But I needed to let my feelings be known."

Drexel steepled his fingers in front of him on the table. Clearly, the woman had some sort of delusions about her opinion mattering to anyone in the room. Nevertheless, Drex was slowly starting to put the puzzle pieces together to form a comprehensive picture. Starting with that easy corner piece. That piece being how well he knew his brother.

She really was quite attractive. It didn't take a genius to surmise that his brother must have indulged in one last dalliance before his impending nuptials. And now the codallier was too enthralled and smitten to see Chase tie himself to another woman.

Chase never did make anything easy on himself. Or on Drexel for that matter.

"Objections are usually reserved for the ceremony, are they not?" he asked. "When the officiant asks whether there are any. You know, *Speak now or forever*…well, you know." Not that doing it that way would have been less disruptive. But Drex was trying to get a feel for what exactly her thinking was.

Another brisk shake of her head. "Of course I know. But I'm not invited to the wedding. I have to do it now."

Drexel couldn't help the curious spark of admiration he felt at her answer. She was determined to go through with this calamity, despite how nervous she clearly was. "I see."

She forged ahead. "Obviously, no one has to listen. And obviously, people have the right to do what they want." She motioned to his brother and his bride. "But I have to say my piece. And hope someone listens."

"And that is what, exactly?"

Maybe he was being too indulgent: he really should politely but firmly take her by the elbow and escort her out at this point. But heaven help him, he wanted to hear what she had to say.

Clairey tried to clamp down on her nervousness. She hadn't expected another person to be in the room, but he was clearly in charge. The others seated around the table seemed to think so, anyway. They were all staring at him, waiting for his direction. Even the bride and groom themselves.

"Ms. Robi," he prompted her now.

Oh, yes, he'd asked her a question, hadn't he? What was it again? Seeming to sense her struggle, he repeated it. "Perhaps you'd like to tell us exactly what your concerns are with regard to this union." He motioned to the couple seated across him.

Clairey noticed for the first time the wide-eyed panic in the bride's eyes. She'd gone a marble shade of pale. The look she directed at Clairey was clear: *Please don't do this.*

Once again, Clairey felt the inklings of doubt and hesitated. She didn't want to ruin anyone's reputation, but the things the bride had told he last night in her drunken state could not be ignored in good conscience. Still, she wasn't going to divulge the other woman's ramblings outright. She had to tread carefully here.

She licked her lips, which had suddenly gone desert-dry. She scrambled to find the right combination of words. The things the bride had told her last night had been divulged in confidence, as awful as they were. Clairey hated to think she was betraying that confidence, but what choice did she have?

As common a cliché as the horrible stepmother was in various fairy tales and folklore, life was more complicated than that. Danielle really seemed to be in over her head as far as the prospect of parenting a young child.

Unlike Clairey's own stepparent, the woman didn't seem to harbor real ill will. Rather, Clairey sensed she was nervous and apprehensive about the vast responsibility about to be foisted on her.

"Um… I don't think the couple have thought through exactly what a life change marriage might be for everyone involved. *Everyone.*"

Dear God, she knew she sounded downright ditzy.

A peal of laughter erupted from the bride's mother. The photographer coughed into his hand. As loud as it all was, Clairey could hear the nervous breathing from Danielle.

Clairey swallowed and forced herself to continue. "It takes more than a wedding ceremony to make someone a stepparent. I'm not sure the couple has thought that through." It was as close to specific as she was willing to get at the moment in front of everyone.

"This is ridiculous," the bride's mother declared. "Drexel, surely you don't intend to indulge this…this…twit any longer."

Ouch. That one hit home. Being called names was nothing new for her. She'd been called that and many other similar slurs throughout the years. Only, right now, she did feel rather like a twit. Albeit a twit with good intentions.

"Look," she began, "I just think these two would be better off maybe rethinking the wedding. I would just hate to see anyone hurt." Particularly one five-year-old girl with strawberry-red corkscrew curls and a wide smile with two missing teeth.

The man who called himself Drexel rose slightly in his chair at her last word. "What do you mean by *hurt*?"

She should have used a different word. She clearly had his attention. Before, he'd been eyeing her with a mild curiosity. But there was nothing mild about the expression he had right now.

At her silence, he added, "That's quite a thing

to say, Miss Robi. Surely, you don't mean *hurt* in the physical sense?"

"No!" she answered right away. Though there really wasn't any way to be certain, now, was there?

Besides, physical hurt wasn't the only way a child could be severely damaged. As she knew firsthand.

Someone in the room swore; another released an exasperated sigh. Neither one being the groom. Surprisingly, he wasn't saying much at all, just glancing over at his brother as if seeking guidance. For heaven's sake, the man couldn't even come up with anything to say. He really had no business getting married without considering all the ramifications.

Clairey summoned all the courage she could muster. She had to get through this. "I've simply ascertained, over the course of my dealings with both the bride and groom throughout the week, that perhaps they are rushing into this marriage. I'm not sure either one has really thought it through. And there is a child to consider in all this."

Drexel's eyebrows rose ever so slightly.

The bride's mother shot up out of her chair, so abruptly that she nearly knocked it over behind her. "I'll hear no more of this nonsense. I don't know why anyone here is indulging this woman." She shot an accusing glare in Drexel's direction. "She should be shown the door. I will have no part of it." Huffing, she stormed out of the room.

The bride's eyes darted from her mother's retreating back, then to Clairey, as if debating whether to follow. Seemingly making a decision, she stood and caught up to the older woman. Before walking through the door, she turned with both hands on her hips. "I don't know what this is, but it's obvious Clairey is not exactly credible. I wouldn't believe a word that comes out of her mouth." With that, she stormed off after her mother, leaving the door wide open.

Clairey almost guffawed out loud at that last statement. Danielle had sounded very different about her last night. In a drunken stupor, she'd been slurring her words as she unloaded about how much she didn't want to become a stepmother. That she didn't even particularly like the groom's five-year-old daughter from a previous relationship. She didn't like children in general and really resented having to be saddled with a child for the rest of her life simply because she was marrying its father. *Its* being the actual word Danielle had used.

But all that was almost secondary. The really troublesome thing, as far as Clairey was concerned, was the clear animosity in her voice and in her eyes as she talked about the girl. Marnie

as an innocent and unsuspecting child. She
had no real say in any of this. No voice at all.

Clairey had no idea who or where the girl's biological mother was. But it was clear the woman was not involved in the child's life whatsoever.

In that way, she might have considered herself lucky. At least Clairey had enjoyed the benefit of having both parents in her life for the early part of it. Before everything had fallen apart and her life had shattered when she'd least expected. Clairey pushed the memories away. This wasn't about her.

No, Marnie had no one who really seemed to be concerned about her welfare. No one to speak up on her behalf.

So Clairey would have to do it.

Despite the two dramatic exits, it appeared the strange little standoff continued. Drexel glanced at his watch. He was due on a conference call with a client overseas in under an hour. And this conversation, as unbelievable as it was, seemed to be going nowhere.

Quickly signing his name on the last check—there was no real indication that the wedding would be called off, after all—he rose from his seat.

As Drexel expected, Chase immediately followed his lead and stood as well. The photographer still sat with his mouth agape. The poor

man hadn't said a thing since this Clairey ha
barged in. Drexel pushed the last check in hi
direction across the table to reassure him that h
would indeed be getting paid despite the strang
call to cancel the wedding.

Not that it had any credence. But somethin
had compelled Ms. Clairey Robi to do wha
she just did. Drexel had always trusted his in
stincts. They'd served him well and had gotte
him rather far in life. If there was anything he'
learned throughout his adult years, it was tha
he should heed his gut feelings.

His intuition was telling him to get to the bot
tom of whatever had caused all of this drama
She'd mentioned concern for Marnie, his niece
That was worrisome.

But for now, it was high time to end this. Thi
meeting was neither the time nor place for it
Though, he'd have to find Clairey Robi at som
point and figure out exactly what had her so ag
itated about his brother's wedding.

What exactly had she meant about Chase and
his bride not being ready to coparent? How in
the world would she possibly know that? Wa:
it just some kind of a ruse to cover her true mo-
tives?

Again, it occurred to him she was yet another
of Chase's jilted flings. But something about
that theory didn't sit right the more he studied
her right now. For one, she'd barely glanced in

his brother's direction this whole time. They hadn't so much as made eye contact, not that he'd seen from where he was sitting.

Which would be rather odd if a wayward fling was the reason for the woman's outburst. No, upon further reflection, Drexel was almost certain he could rule out that this scenario might be due to an ill-timed love affair. For some strange reason, that brought an odd sense of relief coursing through him.

Which made no sense. It really was none of his business if his brother had indulged in one last rendezvous before tying himself to one woman for the rest of his life.

Though, heaven knew, for Drexel even the very idea nearly made him break out in hives.

To each his own.

He crossed his arms in front of his chest and leveled his gaze on Clairey who was now chewing her bottom lip quite aggressively. She was certain to draw blood at any moment.

"You've said your piece, Ms. Robi. I believe you should leave now, as I need to go about my day."

A flash of clear anger shone in her eyes. "Are you dismissing me? Like some sort of—"

"Employee of the hotel?" he finished for her. As callous as his words were, Drexel really had more pressing matters to deal with. He just didn't have time for her anymore. Not if she

wasn't going to be specific about what she w.
here to say. "Precisely."

She bristled and uttered something under h
breath. He'd barely made it out but suspecte
she'd called him a rather unseemly body pa
Without another word, she turned on her he
and stormed out of the room.

Everyone remaining in the room stared s
lently at the door after she'd left. Feeling uncon
fortable, someone cleared their throat. Suddenl
Chase bolted out of his seat.

"I'm going to go find Danielle."

Not so fast. Drexel stopped his brother's ex
with a raise of his hand. "Hold on for a minu
there, bro. I'd say we need to have a chat."

The others in the room apparently took that a
a sign for their own departure. One by one, the
gathered their things and took their leave, utte
ing excuses about having to be somewhere els

What a mess!

His brother started to protest as soon as the
were alone. "I'd really like to go find Danielle
She's bound to be upset after what just hap
pened."

Drexel clicked the tip of his pen up and dow
"What exactly just happened, Chase?"

His brother released an exasperated huf
"You think I know? I have no idea why tha
confounded woman just did what she did."

"None whatsoever? No idea at all what migl

have compelled her to barge in on a private meeting and make the declaration that she made?"

Chase merely shook his head, his eyes wide.

"Think hard, little bro. Is there anything that might have triggered her actions?" He paused before adding, "Perhaps there was something you did to trigger them?"

Chase blinked at him. "You think I'm responsible for this?"

"I'm merely asking."

"You're asking in a very accusatory way there, brother."

"She's very attractive."

His brother's eyebrows snapped together. "Yeah? So? What's that got to do with anything?"

Drex sighed and pinched the bridge of his nose. Nothing was ever smooth or easy when it came to his little brother. Not even a simple prewedding meeting. "Let's start again. Do you have any idea what the woman might have been talking about?"

"What's with the third degree? I already told you I don't know."

Drex ignored that. "Why did she mention your daughter?"

"She happens to be your niece."

Drex was hanging onto his patience by a mere thread. A thread perilously close to snapping at any moment. "Answer the question."

"Look, Danielle's a talker. Maybe she mentioned something to this woman about Marnie."

"What might she have said?"

Chase released a deep sigh. "She's a little apprehensive. About being a stepmom. If you must know."

"Isn't it a little late for that? She knew you were a father when she met you."

Chase shrugged. "Yeah. But Marnie was with Mom most of the time back then. Her being with me full-time is rather new."

Drexel felt the now-familiar pang of loss and sadness settle deep in his gut at the mention of their mother. Up until several weeks ago, Alice Osoman had been a fairly active woman. One that could take care of her granddaughter despite her disease. She'd been managing her relatively mild symptoms well enough. Then she suddenly got worse. Now she was merely a shell of her former self. A shell who probably wouldn't even recognize the girl anymore. The doctors were very sympathetic when they'd explained that she had one of the rare cases of the disease that progressed particularly rapidly.

That was an understatement. It was as if her symptoms had magnified overnight.

Drex pushed away the distressing thoughts and turned his attention back to his sibling. "If that's the case, then I dare say this Miss Robi was right."

Chase's shoulders slumped, and he rubbed his eyes.

Drex continued, not ready to spare any sympathy given the import of the matter. "You need to figure this out before you and your bride say your *I do*s."

CHAPTER TWO

WELL, THAT HAD gone well. *Not!*

Clairey plopped down in her office chair and waited for the inevitable reckoning. Sure enough, mere seconds later, a loud knocking sounded from the other side of the door. Actually, *pounding* would be a better word. Louis didn't bother waiting for an answer before barging into the room.

"Clairissa! What in the world did you just do? Are you out of your mind?"

Clairey made certain to not so much as flinch. She wouldn't cower. And she certainly wouldn't apologize. She'd made her decision and had acted on it. She would lie in the bed she'd made.

"What in heaven's name were you thinking?" Louis demanded to know. "To interfere in a paid event! A wedding, no less."

She swallowed, lifted her chin and looked the man straight in the eye. "I had my reasons."

He scoffed dismissively. "That's all you have to say for yourself?"

"It's all I have."

He glared at her. "Well, it isn't much."

"I'm sorry, Louis." It was all she could say at this point.

His eyes grew wide. "You're sorry? That the bride and her mom both read me the riot act? They want their pound of flesh for what you just pulled."

"I had no doubt that they would."

"Did you? Did you really think it through? Did you consider that they would trash us online with negative reviews? That they would consider suing and demand refunds? Because that's exactly what they threatened to do."

Clairey squeezed her eyes shut. Louis had a right to be angry. None of this was his fault in any way. She couldn't very well do much about the litigation part. "I'll respond to each online comment. And I'll post on every travel site that it was all me."

He pointed a thick, stubby finger in her direction. "That's not going to do squat, and you know it. We'll be dealing with the fallout from your foolish actions for months to come. Maybe years."

"I'm sorry," she repeated, completely at a loss for anything else to say. She certainly wasn't about to get into her motivations for acting so rashly. Or how much of a kinship she'd felt for

the little girl involved. Clairey hadn't even confided more than the bare basics of her childhood
to Tessa. She certainly wasn't about to confide
in her furious boss.

Anyway, something told her Louis wasn't
the type who would understand. There'd be no
sense in explaining to him that the cliché of the
evil stepmother could be all too true in real life.
Or stepfather, in her case.

He ignored her apology. "And apparently the
brother is some type of hotshot businessman
with considerable clout. The very type of person
who can ruin a business with a couple of phone
calls to his myriad of friends in high places.
Even a place like a high-end resort in Cape Cod,
Massachusetts, that's been around for years."

"Then, you have no choice but to place the
blame squarely on a low-level employee, I suppose."

Louis rubbed his eyes. "You bet I will. Not
that it will do much good."

Clairey hadn't any doubt his plan had been to
do just that all along—throw her to the wolves.
"I really am sorry," she repeated. "I did what I
thought was right."

He shook his head. "Huh. Pack up your desk.
In case there was any doubt, you're fired."
Sneering at her, he turned away. He slammed
the door on his way out, hard enough that her
smock fell off the hook. Not that she'd be need-

ng it any longer. As activities manager, one
f her duties was to come up with crafts and
ther ways to keep the younger resort guests oc-
upied and happy. This morning's activity had
een to paint paper kites, then try to fly them
n the beach. She'd really miss that particular
art of the job.

Clairey inhaled and resisted the urge to give
n to the sting of tears behind her eyes. She
ould do any crying once she'd packed up all
er stuff and got out of here. She'd be darned
f Louis, or anyone else for that matter, might
appen to return and see her cry.

She was impulsive and reckless, and what had
gotten her in the end? She'd only managed to
eopardize the reputation of the resort and the
bs of her coworkers, who happened to be some
f her dearest friends. Not to mention, she hadn't
hanged anyone's mind. The wedding was sure
o go forward.

Maybe she could talk to the brother. Drexel.
he hotshot businessman. Explain to him why
he'd done what she had. Convince him not to
etaliate. After all, she'd only been doing what
he thought was right. She'd been trying to pro-
ect his very own niece. Did he know how re-
entful his soon-to-be sister-in-law felt about
ecoming a stepmother? He would see her rea-
oning when she explained. No doubt he would

try to dismiss her. But Clairey would find a wa
to make him understand.

Though, she had no clue how to go abo
doing that. There was no time. In a matter o
minutes, she would be escorted out of here b
one of the resort's security personnel. Louis wa
probably at the guard shed by the entrance rig
now, posting her picture on the wall with clea
instructions that she never get past the gate ev
again.

No. Clairey wasn't going to be able to expla
anything: she'd probably never see Mr. Drex
Osoman again. It wasn't as if they ran in th
same circles.

But she had to try. A little girl's well-bein
depended on it.

Drexel was distracted. More than a little. U
characteristically so. A pretty sorry state of a
fairs, given how much he had to get done toda
and how far behind he was. It also didn't hel
matters that he was completely out of his usua
environment. Trying to work on internationa
deals while stranded on a family-oriented reso
was challenging, to say the least. And *strande*
was the perfect way to describe his situation a
far as he was concerned. He'd commissione
use of one of the main conference rooms and s
up a temporary office but still found it hard t
concentrate. Every few moments or so, a shrie

ing child would run down the hallway outside or a service person would run a vacuum in the hallway while he was trying to update a spreadsheet or manage an overseas call.

One of those calls came through at that very moment. His potential deal partner calling from Abu Dhabi, Sheikh Farhan.

Drex sighed with resignation and tapped to accept the call. The man barely gave him a chance to say hello before beginning to speak.

"Haven't heard from you in a while, my friend. Was wondering if you would even answer the phone."

They'd spoken less than forty-eight hours ago.

"Just getting ready to attend and celebrate my younger brother's nuptials."

"Ah, yes, the wedding. Please send our family's congratulations to your brother."

"Thank you. I will let him know."

He was back to business immediately. Not that Drex could blame him. A lot was riding on their potential collaboration. For him especially. Much more so than the sheikh. "You'll be available for the conference call on Tuesday, correct?" he asked Drex, not for the first time.

"Absolutely," Drex reassured him. "With updated documents and figures for you to go over beforehand."

Mollified for the moment, the sheikh bade him goodbye and hung up.

Drexel leaned back in his chair and sighed. Despite what he'd just told Sheikh Farhan, he wasn't fooling himself. He *was* having trouble focusing at the moment. He cursed himself for it internally. Given the importance of this deal, he couldn't afford to botch it up now. He'd come too far in life, accomplished too much, to risk a deal of this magnitude falling through.

The real reason he couldn't concentrate was because he couldn't get a certain wavy-haired brunette out of his mind. The determination in her voice, the rigid set of her spine. The strength blazing behind her eyes. Every time he tried to answer an email or focus on a new development, his mind started wandering to Clairey Robi and exactly what her motivation had been.

Chase might have acted offended when he'd been questioning him, but they both knew that what Drexel was asking him was not beyond the realm of possibility.

But he'd been right. Chase and this Clairey hadn't actually been romantically or physically involved. Or in any way, for that matter. She'd said she was worried about Chase's daughter. Why exactly was she so invested? Was it simply out of the goodness of her heart? If that was the case, she would truly be a rare breed. Most people didn't stick their necks out for others they didn't even know. Not even for children.

If Chase's bride and her mother had anything

to say about it, the young lady would find herself in the unemployment line. Yet, she'd taken that risk without hesitation. Heaven knew, Drex himself hadn't met many such people in his lifetime. Most people turned a blind eye or pretended not to notice when something was amiss in a household.

Not Clairey Robi.

He was more curious about her than he could explain or wanted to examine.

When was the last time he'd found himself so intrigued by a woman? If it had ever happened before, he couldn't remember.

An email marked *Urgent* popped up on his laptop screen, but this time he knew better than to try to address it. With a curse, he slammed the cover shut and stood. Technically, he was on vacation, after all. Not that any of his colleagues or clients were heeding that fact. Several matters required his immediate attention, but he knew when to call it a day. He wasn't going to get anything done until he found her.

A brief visit to the front desk told him exactly where to find Ms. Robi's office. "But I'd hurry if I was you. She won't be there long," the desk attendant warned him before he left.

Apparently, Drexel was right about that too. Her antics this morning had indeed gotten her fired.

Her desk was packed up. Nothing left to do now but turn in her badge and leave. A knock sounded on the door as Clairey took one last look around the small office. For one insane moment, she had the heartwarming thought that perhaps Louis had changed his mind. But no such luck. The person who opened the door a moment later was Matt, the bar manager who also happened to be her rather casual boyfriend. If she could call him that. Well, they'd gone on more than a few dates. But Matt had made it clear they were not exclusive. More than clear, in fact. Yeah, he definitely wouldn't consider himself her boyfriend. Especially not now, when she was unemployed and completely broke.

"So, you heard," she said as he stepped inside the room.

"Yeah. Sorry, babe. But what were you thinking?"

"I've been asking myself that all day. Oh, and Louis wanted an answer too."

"He came into the bar area after. Red as a beet and mumbling under his breath."

"He does that when he's angry."

"Then, he's downright incensed. Did you really try to stop the Osoman/Traynor wedding? Barged in on them in the conference room?"

Clairey felt her chin tremble. When he put it that way, what she'd done sounded super unreasonable. "I'll tell you all about it over dinner tonight at the Crab Shack."

Matt ducked his head. "Yeah…um…about at."

Oh, no. She should have seen this coming. att wasn't exactly the loyal type. He had more an a healthy concern about each of them pay-g equally whenever they went out. And now at she was out of a job…

"I forgot there was something I had to do to-ght. Sorry. Totally slipped my mind."

Right. What a lousy liar.

She'd been right. Matt wanted no part of her ow that she was unemployed. Said a lot about er worth in his eyes. The chin tremble sud-enly got worse.

She wasn't surprised. Life had shown her nore than once that people could be quick to irn a cold shoulder. Even those closest to her.

No job. No romantic prospects. No hope of nything getting better anytime soon.

"I understand," she said simply. She cer-inly wasn't about to beg or plead with him to eep their date. She'd seen that sort of desper-te act up close countless times as a teenager. Ier mother never considered herself above beg-ing when it came to her stepfather. Even be-ore they'd gotten married. It still brought tears) her eyes when Clairey remembered all the arious times she'd done so. For a man who lidn't deserve her. A man who had torn their ives apart.

And her stepfather's actions had demonstrated to her just how little Clairey had meant to her remaining parent.

Clairey tossed off the memories and focused back on Matt. "Maybe you should just go," she told him instead.

He shrugged without so much as a pause. "I'd help you carry your stuff out, but I have to head back. The bar is getting slammed 'cause of the rain."

She shook her head. She wouldn't accept his help anyway. Besides, it was only a couple of boxes and her wilted plant. She could be out of here in two trips.

"Then, you should probably just leave, Matt."

He did so without another word. What a day it had turned out to be. She'd lost her job and her boyfriend—who wasn't actually even her boyfriend. So why did she feel like she'd just been kicked when she was already on the ground? Well, it didn't pay to feel sorry for herself. That wasn't going to do anything for her. Clairey blew out a breath and grabbed the bigger box to take to her car. Walking by the front desk, she managed to keep her head high and not make eye contact with any of the other employees. The so-called Walk of Shame. At least no one from Security had shown up to escort her out. If she rushed, she could get out of here without having that added indignity thrust upon her.

Within moments, she was back from the parking lot to grab the remaining box and the precious philodendron which she balanced on the lid. Heavy footsteps sounded in the hallway leading to her office. Clairey bit out a curse.

A security officer, no doubt. She'd taken too long. But there was still a chance she could evade him if she rushed out the other direction. In her haste to leave the room and avoid the newcomer, she turned on her heel. Too fast. The plant went flying off the box and flew in an arch through the air to squarely hit the midsection of the man who'd just appeared at her door.

And it was no security officer. Drexel Osoman stood there covered in soil, a look of utter annoyance on his face.

She had thrown a wet, dirty plant at him! Drexel squelched the urge to swear out loud. It wasn't easy. Before this morning, he'd had no idea this woman even existed; now she was the bane of his existence. She was the reason he'd gotten absolutely no work done today. And she was the reason he was now standing here with mud plastered on his tailored silk shirt.

"Oh, my God!" she cried, still holding the cardboard box. "I'm so sorry. I guess I overwatered it this morning."

Drex looked down at the mess of mud covering his torso. "I'd say."

"It's just that you surprised me. I wasn't e
pecting anyone and—" She eyed him with
narrowed gaze. "What are you doing here, an
way?"

She had to ask?

"I wanted to talk. Do you have a minute?"

Her shoulders slumped in a gesture of con
plete and utter defeat. For just a moment, Dre
felt the slightest bit sorry for her. But then
glob of mud fell off his shirt and landed on h
Italian leather loafers.

"I guess I owe you some answers."

She had that right. He pulled over the cha
sitting in the corner of the room and sat. "Yo
stirred quite the hornet's nest down there ea
lier today."

She dropped the box on her desk and stare
at him. "Did I?"

"Yes. For what it's worth."

"That's the question, isn't it? What was
worth? From where I'm standing, nothing ha
changed. The wedding will go on, won't it?"

"Indeed, it will."

She nodded once. "Right. So the only thin
I managed to accomplish is to steer myself ou
of a job. With no real hope of finding any kin
of adequate replacement."

"Yet, something tells me you'd do the sam
thing if given the opportunity to do it again."

She studied him before answering. "You're

very observant. I was going to try to find a way to contact you. See if you could help. Apparently, you're fairly well-known in certain circles. Not that I had any sort of clue how to go about it."

That surprised him. She was thinking about turning to him with all this? "Why?"

She shrugged. "You were clearly the one in charge in that room. And it wasn't as if the bride's mother was going to be of any help. I'm pretty certain she was ready to toss me into the waves out there." She motioned with her head in the direction of the ocean outside her window.

If he had been curious before, now he was totally intrigued. He wouldn't be able to sleep until he got to the bottom of her motivation for doing what she'd done.

"And what exactly would you have me do?"

She threw her hands in the air. "I don't know. Stop the wedding, at least temporarily. Your brother and his bride have a lot they still haven't considered before tying the knot."

"And you know this how?"

"I suppose I have to tell you."

"Indeed, you do. You said it involved Marnie. My niece."

She rubbed her forehead, expelling a weary sigh. "It does. I was at the bar last night, to visit my boyfriend. Well, not that he was ever really a boyfriend. Which doesn't even matter. He just broke up with me. If one even can break up with someone they weren't really dating. Not technically, as he kept reminding me."

Drex lifted his hand. "If we could stick to the matter at hand?"

"Right. Well, Danielle, your soon-to-be sister-in-law, was sitting there on one of the stools. She'd already indulged quite a bit by the time I got there. I was actually going to recommend to Matt that they cut her off. The Sea View has rules about such things. I can't imagine why they let her continue on the way she did. Just ordering drink after drink. Some of the cocktails were pretty heavy drinks too."

Drexel tried not to let his irritation show. It wasn't easy. "Again, Ms. Robi…"

"Sorry. Well, she started talking about how she was ready to get married but not to be a stepmother."

Ah, so that was indeed the problem. Just as Chase had offered earlier. "I see."

Clairey blinked at him as if expecting him to say more. She went on when he didn't. "She continued about what a brat her future stepdaughter was. Which I don't understand. I've had little Marnie in the activity room all week, and she's an absolute doll. So creative. And full of humor. She makes me laugh at least once a day."

"Ms. Robi," Drexel said to redirect her. It was so very hard to keep this woman on track.

"Oh. Sorry."

"You do realize that all her talk may have just been the drunken ramblings of a completely inebriated woman."

She rolled her eyes at him. "Of course. But she still said those things. After all, doesn't alcohol usually diminish one's inhibitions so deeply that the speaker's truth emerges?"

She had a point there. Not a chance worth taking when a child was involved.

Clairey inhaled deeply, as if bracing herself before going on. "There's more. Danielle said she couldn't wait to find a way to get rid of the child. One way or another."

Drexel released a deep sigh. That was another matter entirely. Being apprehensive was one thing. But if the woman had plans to actually find a way to toss Marnie aside somewhere, it was clearly a serious matter. Marnie was much too young to be displaced once again. The little girl was barely processing the abrupt and unexpected loss of her grandmother as her primary caregiver.

Clairey may have gone about it in a rather reckless way, but she clearly had reason to be concerned. Though, clearly Danielle had overindulged in drink. Maybe all this was much ado about nothing. There was a chance she didn't mean all that she'd said to Clairey last night.

"I know I'm a stranger, but I'd hate to think

that an innocent little girl is about to be thrust into a bad situation and that I did nothing to try and stop it."

Drex had heard enough. "Thank you for your concern, Ms. Robi. Don't give the matter another thought. You've done enough."

She stood abruptly. In a flash, she was at his side and had him by the elbow. The woman could move quickly. Drex's gaze fell to where her small hand rested on his arm. An inexplicable rush of warmth spread over his skin where she touched him. She hastily removed her fingers.

"Wait. You're just going to ignore everything I just told you?"

"On the contrary," he answered. "I'm going to go find my brother." Though, he would stop in his room to change clothes first. "It appears he and I need to have another talk." This time, Drex would demand some real answers.

CHAPTER THREE

HE SHOULD HAVE known things weren't going to go smoothly down here. Matters relating to his brother seldom did. Now, said brother was about to marry a woman who didn't want any part of raising his child. Drexel bypassed the elevator and made his way to the stairs. Even though he was uncomfortable with a mess of mud on his shirt, he figured he'd need some kind of physical exertion after the conversation he'd just had. He didn't know his young niece very well; that was on him. It was too late now, but Drex should have spent more time and effort getting to know his niece. He should have checked in on her well-being after his mom had taken seriously ill. And he should have made sure Chase was adjusting to becoming a full-time parent to an active, curious little girl.

He felt a pang of sympathy for her now. No child deserved to be stranded with someone who didn't want them. How ironic that Chase of all people would put his own daughter in such a predicament, given the way they'd had to grow up. Chase knew all too well how damaging such an existence could be for a child. They both did.

Bad enough the girl's own mother had abandoned her when she'd been barely more than an infant. Chase didn't even know what had become of his former fling. Drexel snorted a humorless laugh as he rounded the stairway turn on the third floor. He wondered if Chase even remembered the woman's full name. The kids these days would call her Chase's baby momma. But heaven knew the woman had never done any kind of momma-ing.

Marnie had mostly been brought up by Chase and Drex's mother up until she'd finally succumbed to the disease that had plagued her for years. His mom couldn't even take care of herself now, let alone a dependent child.

Drex had wondered how Chase would adjust to having his daughter back full-time. Ms. Clairey Robi had just told him the answer. When he finally reached his hallway, Drex could see that he wouldn't have to hunt down his brother, after all. Chase was waiting for him at the door.

Chase looked awful. His hair was a disheveled mess, as if he'd been running his hands through it. Half of his shirttail was untucked and hanging over his hip. His pallor was an odd shade of gray. And he looked nervous. He almost laughed at the spectacle they made together with Drex covered in drying mud and Chase looking as sloppy as he did.

His brother did a double take as he noticed Drex's attire as he approached. "What the heck happened to you?"

"You wouldn't believe me if I told you," Drex answered as he pulled his key card out to unlock the door. "And I could ask you the same question."

"Danielle and I were doing some talking. Things got a little heated."

Another curious turn to the sordid saga. Drex didn't really want to know what their conversation might have been about. But with resignation, he opened the hotel-room door and motioned for his brother to enter.

Chase began speaking immediately, not giving Drexel even the moment it took to take his shirt off to change. "So I need you to take Marnie."

Drexel gave his head a brisk shake. He couldn't have heard him correctly. "I thought Danielle's mother was going to take her until the two of you got back from your honeymoon."

Chase inhaled deeply. "I mean long-term."

Drexel stilled in the process of walking to the washroom to clean up. "Come again?"

Chase thrust his fingers through the hair at his crown. "Danielle came clean about why that resort employee barged into the meeting this morning. It's because Danielle confided in her. About not wanting to be burdened with a kid through marriage."

Drexel knew all that already. But what did any of that have to do with him taking Marnie for any amount of time, let alone long-term?

Studying the desperation clear on Chase's face, the answer began to dawn on him. His brother's bride had given him an ultimatum. And Chase was choosing his bride over his daughter.

"It's probably going to be temporary."

"What makes you think you'll be ready to take her back later? If you don't want to parent her now?"

Chase blinked at him in confusion. "I don't mean me."

"Then, who?"

He shrugged. "I mean, Mom might recover and take her back, right? You've got her set up with the top doctors in one of the most renowned institutions in the country to make sure she gets the best care."

Drex closed his eyes briefly. Chase knew better. Was he trying to fool himself, or did he take his older brother for a fool?

"You know she's not going to get better."

Chase looked down at his shoes. "Then, you can set Marnie up with a slew of nannies."

Drexel knew he shouldn't be surprised. Much

too often in their life, his younger brother had shown himself to be an utterly selfish and narcissistic type. Maybe Drexel was a fool for ever expecting anything different from his younger sibling.

He could kick himself for not having seen this coming.

"You have to do this, man," Chase said, his voice tight yet determined. "There is no one else. You have to take her."

Clairey knew she was tempting fate. If she was smart, she'd be off this resort by now. Her office was packed up and locked. All that was left to do was to surrender her employee badge and walk out the double doors of the entrance.

But she couldn't bring herself to leave without stopping by the kids' activity room just one last time. The hours she'd spent in there had been the best part of her job, the responsibility she would miss the most by far, now that it was all over. The smiling faces of those kids as they painted or danced or worked on various crafts had brought joy to her days. She'd take the company of the children over the adult resort guests any day. Spending time with those children reminded her of the good times from her own childhood. Before it had all fallen apart with the tragic loss that had changed everything. And now she was losing that forever.

To her surprise, a parent strode into the room with a tot in tow, followed by another mother with her son. And then a dad trailed by with a set of twin boys. They each sat down at a station and stared at her expectantly.

Louis hadn't even thought to cancel the afternoon's crafting class. Well, she wasn't about to disappoint all the kids who'd shown up. There was no way Louis would set security on her when she was entertaining a roomful of children. And besides, she may have been technically fired, but she was on the clock until the end of day. Louis had told her this was the last date of her employment. No one had said anything about the hour it was to end.

As she greeted the children, another girl ran into the room and took a seat at one of the stations up front: Marnie.

Clairey hadn't even seen who had brought her down. Usually, Danielle or her mother did it. Neither one stuck around after dropping the child off. No different today. Now, the little girl gave her a wide smile and a small wave.

A dull pain throbbed in Clairey's chest at what the poor child might be dealing with in a few short days. She could only hope Drex had talked to his brother and found some kind of resolution.

Drex.

Since when had she considered herself fa-

miliar enough with the man to think of him
by a shortened moniker? She cringed inwardly
thinking about the way she'd accidentally flung
a plant pot full of mud in his direction and made
a mess of his shirt. Somehow, he'd still managed
to look distinguished and handsome, despite
being covered in mud. For an insane moment,
she'd thought he might take his shirt off and
give her a look at what was sure to be a chiseled, muscular chest.

Clairey gave her head a brisk shake. What
was wrong with her? She had a class to run
here, had no business thinking about Drexel
Osoman's looks or the way he might look shirt-
less.

Half an hour later, the children were elbow-
deep in molding clay. Most of the parents had
chosen to leave, so Clairey did her best to bestow ample attention to each child as they at-
tempted their foray into the art of sculpting.
Though, she couldn't seem to help hovering
over Marnie just a bit more than the others.

She sensed him before she saw him.

Sure enough, when Clairey looked up, Drexel
Osoman was standing in the hallway outside
the classroom. She had to suck in a breath at
the sight of him. Though he was dressed much
more casually than when she'd first seen him
this morning, the man still emitted a clear aura
of authority and command. No wonder every-

one in that room this morning had been waiting for him to decide their cue.

He wore a short-sleeved Henley shirt that brought out the contours of his clearly muscular chest. No one should look that formidable in pressed khakis. A silver and gold watch adorned his left wrist. Heavens! How was she supposed to get through the remaining minutes of her class with him standing out there looking so very…masculine?

Curiosity had her chest tightening. Why was he the one here for Marnie?

Finally, the hour was up, and parents slowly trickled in to pick up their children. Marnie made a beeline for her uncle as soon as she saw him. Drexel looked hesitant as the child hugged him around the knees, as if unsure how exactly to greet her.

"Hey, sport," he said, tousling her hair. That earned him a wide grin.

"I made a bunny rabbit!" She pointed to the glob of clay at her desk that resembled nothing akin to a bunny rabbit.

"I see that. Well done!" Drexel told her, the corners of his mouth lifted.

Clairey forced away her trepidation and made herself walk to where they stood. She had no reason to feel so anxious around him. She didn't even know the man, for Pete's sake. Still, everyone else had gone, and she was essentially

one with him—the presence of Marnie not-
withstanding.

She cleared her throat before she could say
hello. And there was something else she wanted
say to him. "I wanted to thank you," she
blurted out before she lost the nerve.

"For?"

"For caring enough to find me earlier. For
asking why I did what I did."

Marnie, seemingly bored with the conversation, left them to go play some more with her
mound of clay at her station.

Drexel lifted his chin. "You're welcome. I'm
glad you told me."

"And?"

He crossed his arms in front of his chest.
"You're wondering how my conversation with
my brother went."

She nodded. "Yes. Has the situation about
Marnie been resolved?"

His lips tightened before he answered. "Not
exactly."

His instincts were kicking into gear again.
They'd been triggered when he'd walked down
to pick up his niece and seen Clairey with the
children. Chase had flat out announced that
Drex might as well be the one to do it, seeing
as he'd be her guardian soon. Not that Drexel

had willingly agreed, exactly. But for all practical purposes, he had to, didn't he?

What choice did he have? He couldn't very well allow his niece to fall into the foster system just because her father was a dolt. Sure, there were plenty of foster families out there who were kind, caring and competent. But he knew from personal experience it was no way to live. Bouncing around from home to home, never truly belonging in any. The experience could be soul-crushing. Plus, there were also those families who had no business taking in a child. He and Chase had been bounced around to enough of those. No, Marnie wouldn't go into the system if Drex had anything to say about it.

Nor could he risk demanding that Chase man up to his parental responsibilities and keep Marnie, thereby leaving her with two people who resented her existence. Nothing damaged a child more than dealing with parents who resented them. As he very well knew.

There was really only one viable option. He would have to take her and make sure she was okay. He just had to get her situated with a competent nanny. But that was going to take time. And time was a precious resource he didn't have much of at the moment. There were a million things requiring his immediate attention as soon as he returned to his penthouse apartment back in Manhattan. The deal with Sheikh Farhan was currently at a tipping point. What Drex managed to accomplish in the next few weeks would be crucial to its success. Or failure.

He didn't have a spare moment, let alone the amount of time and effort it would take to locate and interview qualified candidates for a reputable nanny. He glanced over at his niece. The youngster was about to lose yet another parent. Kids were resilient, but Marnie was well aware of the fact that she didn't have a momma. And her *mimi* had suddenly been taken away from her. Now, the only father she knew was about to walk away from her as well. Drex knew Marnie was particularly sharp so he couldn't rush this process. He had to make sure to get it right for her sake.

The woman standing before him may very well be the answer to the quandary he'd so recently found himself in. She might be the key to it all, in fact.

"Listen, can I buy you lunch?"

She blinked at him in confusion. "Lunch?"

He almost wanted to laugh at her expression. Clearly, she hadn't seen that coming. Frankly, neither had he up until a few moments ago, when he'd watched her with Marnie and the other children. Every one of them seemed to adore her. She'd certainly held their attention, no small feat with a group of toddlers.

"Yeah. It's typically the midday meal." He

made a show of looking at his watch. "And
happens to be midday."

She rolled her eyes. "I know what lunch i
What I don't know is why you'd ask me to jo
you."

"You'd be joining me and Marnie both. Sl
clearly has a fondness for you. I think she'd li
it if you came along." That was the absolu
truth. He would get into his ulterior motiv
later over the meal.

Her eyes traveled to where Marnie sat gent
holding her ostensible bunny. They held cle
hesitation and no small amount of suspicion.

"Come on, let me buy you lunch. It's the lea
I can do for the way you tried to stick up for n
niece earlier."

She scoffed. "Not that it did any good."

She had no idea. Well, he was about to tell h
exactly what her actions had led to. And exact
how she could play a part in going about fixir
things for the girl. As well as for him.

As if on cue, Marnie suddenly dropped h
art project on the desk. The clay landed wit
a resounding thud. "Uncle Drex, I'm hungry.

Maybe it was low of him, but he would us
her declaration to his advantage. "How abo
some pizza?" A hungry child could be a pov
erful motivator for anyone.

Marnie nodded enthusiastically. Drex
walked over and lifted her into his arms. "I'

asked Ms. Clairey to join us. What do you think of that?"

Marnie clapped her hands. "Yeah! Miss Clairey can come too!"

Clairey tilted her head and gave him a clearly knowing expression. "Why do I get the feeling I've just been played here?"

"Did it work?"

She sighed and brushed back her hair with her fingers. "I suppose it did. I'll come to lunch with you two, but only because Marnie would like me to."

Well, that was a bit of a bruise for the old ego. She walked over and tickled Marnie under the chin, earning a peal of giggles. The scent of Clairey tickled his nose. An enticing scent of roses that reminded him of the first days of spring.

"It has to be off the resort, though. I'm not really supposed to be here."

"Say no more." He held his elbow out to her, Marnie still tucked in the crook of his other arm. "My car is out front."

Less than fifteen minutes later, they were being seated at a homey, rustic Italian restaurant that Clairey had directed him to.

"This place has the best pizza on the peninsula. If not the entire state of Massachusetts," she said, unfolding her napkin and placing it on her lap. Marnie sat next to both of them in a booster seat.

Drex couldn't remember the last time he'd had pizza. When he went out, it was usually to Michelin-star restaurants to entertain clients. Otherwise, he was heating up a prepared meal late at night or grabbing a granola bar at his desk. Meals out at restaurants often were simply to negotiate a deal or acquire new business.

Not that this was any different. Despite having a five-year-old in tow, this was simply yet another business meeting—one he had to close. So much depended on it.

Not unlike his other pending negotiation with the sheikh.

Their waiter arrived and poured them some water. Clairey took a sip before speaking. "So. Let's have it, then. What's this little lunch outing really about? I'm guessing I'm not usually the type of woman you ask out, so what's up?"

She was sharp. And direct. He wasn't sure how to respond to the second part of her question. What she'd said was accurate. Drexel usually did date more glamorous types. His last fling had involved a well-known actress he'd accompanied to Cannes. But the relationship had gone sour when he'd refused to drop everything to attend every movie premiere and red-carpet event she wanted him by her side for. No, Clairey didn't strike him as the type to demand ultimatums.

In that sense at least, she wasn't his usual type.

Clairey had to wait to get her answer. The waiter chose that moment to come to take their orders. They went with the house special, a margherita pizza loaded with basil and lots of fresh, home-made mozzarella. For Marnie, her uncle ordered a small cheese pizza off the children's menu along with a bowl of applesauce.

Normally, simply being in this place made Clairey's mouth water. But she was much too distracted right now to be thinking about the food. Her gut told her this little outing was about more than discussing how Drexel's conversation with his brother had gone. As curious as she was about what had transpired during their conversation, she couldn't very well argue that it was really any of her business. So why exactly was she here?

"So tell me," she prodded once again after the waiter had left. "Why'd you ask me here? I'm guessing you have a slew of eager women who'd be ready to jump at a chance to have lunch with you. You're a handsome, successful man."

He gave her a mischievous smile. "Are you coming on to me, Ms. Robi?"

A flash of heat rushed to her cheeks. "What?

Of course not! I would never do such a thing." Why in the world had she just said all that?

He dramatically clasped his hand on his chest. "You scar my ego yet again." Clairey didn't know what he meant about *again*.

"Relax. It was a joke," he added, taking another bite of his pizza. "Apparently a rather poor one." Clairey was still too nervous to eat. Although, she had no real idea why.

Drexel's next words did nothing to alleviate her anxiety. "I asked you here because I want to discuss a proposition I have for you."

Her skin began to tingle in alarm. She couldn't fathom what kind of proposition he might be referring to.

"You asked how it went when I spoke to my brother earlier. About his bride's reluctance to become a stepmother."

She could only nod.

He let out a long, weary sigh before answering. "The gist of it is that I'm now my niece's sole guardian."

Clairey didn't bother to hide her surprise. The pieces started to fall into place. Drexel's brother had tossed his young daughter aside in order to please his bride. Clairey glanced at the little girl. A smudge of marinara sauce marked her chin. She had applesauce all over her fingers. How could anyone turn their back on such an dorable child? A pang tugged inside her chest. Poor Marnie.

"I see," Clairey answered, though she didn't really. Danielle's position was tough enough to comprehend. She couldn't understand for the life of her how anyone could do such a thing to their own child. But she knew. All too well. She had a very good idea about not being wanted by your only parent.

Drexel continued. "There is no one else. Marnie was being looked after by our mother until very recently, and she isn't able to do so anymore. So it's up to me now." A flash of pain shone in his eyes, and he looked off to the side.

"That's a lot to ask of you."

He shrugged. "Let's just say I'm used to cleaning up my brother's messes. And really, what choice do I have?"

"I'm really sorry, Drexel," Clairey said because it seemed an appropriate thing to say given what he'd just had thrust upon him.

"Thank you."

"But I still don't understand what any of that has to do with me."

"Until I can find an acceptable nanny, I need someone to help me take care of her. I don't know the first thing about parenting a kindergartner."

Clairey's mouth went dry. He couldn't be asking her what she thought he was asking.

"Wait. Are you saying you'd like me to do it?'

He nodded once, his gaze fully fixed on he face. "I'll make it worth your while. She alread knows and likes you."

"But I'm not a child caregiver. I'm a manage at a resort." At least she was up until a coupl of hours ago. "I'm not qualified."

"On the contrary. I saw you with those kid today. You were great with them."

She shook her head. He had to see how wron; this all was. "Leading the activity room wasn' really part of my responsibilities. I simply too! it over because no one else wanted to do it, an(I enjoyed it."

He smiled at her. "That sort of proves m\ point that you're good with kids, wouldn't you say?"

She'd walked right into that one. Drexe leaned closer to her over the table. "I'm guess ing you went through a background check witl the proper authorities before being allowed t(run a children's activity room."

"Yes, but—"

He cut her off. "That already makes one task easier for me. I just have to verify with the re sort rather than go through the whole proces: myself."

He'd really thought of everything. How' She hadn't even laid eyes on the man until thi morning.

"And you do happen to be out of a job," he added, throwing out the proverbial ace card.

He was certainly right about that. Not only was she unemployed now, she had no idea how to go about finding another position anytime soon. The resort had been her first real job out of college. Any prospective employer would be curious as to why it had ended so soon. Louis wasn't going to be of any help with a reference on her behalf either. She had loans and bills and no other source of income whatsoever.

Still, this wasn't right. She felt disoriented by his ask, not sure how to respond.

He was asking her out of desperation, not because he really even wanted her for the role. She should just say no.

Marnie dropped her pizza to the ground with splat and leaned over to stare at it. "Uh-oh. My pizza fell down." She looked up to give Clairey a gummy grin, her lips smudged with red sauce. Another pang tugged in Clairey's chest.

"I'll have to think about it," she answered instead.

CHAPTER FOUR

"PLEASE TALK ME out of this," Clairey told h[e]
friend as she adjusted her helmet and climbe[d]
on her bicycle. It was the perfect day for a lon[g,]
peaceful bike ride. Not too hot or steamy, th[e]
air light with a cool ocean breeze. Cape Co[d]
had miles and miles of pristine bike paths th[at]
afforded some of the most breathtaking scene[s]
of the ocean and various ponds and lakes. [It]
was one of the few activities one could do on [a]
budget around these parts. All you needed w[as]
a rented bike and a bottle full of ice-cold wate[r.]

Tessa gave her a pointed look before pushin[g]
off on her left pedal. "I'll do no such thing," sh[e]
threw over her shoulder as they began to rid[e.]
"You've been handed a golden opportunity ju[st]
when you thought you were down-and-out. Yo[u]
should be thanking the man," she added.

They rode in silence side by side for sever[al]
moments before Clairey found the courage t[o]
admit what was really nagging at her abou[t]

Drexel's offer. "There's something I haven't shared with you about all this," she began.

"What's that?"

She was just going to come out and tell her. "I feel so disoriented around the man. Out of my element. Working for him is bound to be awkward."

Tessa shrugged. "You're attracted to him. I've seen the man. Who can blame you? He's devilishly handsome."

Clairey didn't have it in her to argue that. She'd be lying.

"Besides," Tessa added, "you wouldn't be the first woman to be attracted to a drop-dead gorgeous employer."

"I suppose not."

"I know you're a true professional who can handle it."

If only she could be sure of that. That point was precisely where all her doubts lay. She could easily imagine making a fool of herself over someone like Drexel Osoman. Not to mention, the little girl in his care was already well on her way to capturing Clairey's heart.

After they'd ridden about three miles, Tessa motioned to pull over. Clairey wasn't surprised. They'd been on enough rides together that she knew this was typically the point when Tessa would need a break. They pulled up next to a wooden park bench that faced an opening in the greenery with a perfect view of a small swamp pond. A family of five was crabbing in the water with plastic pails and small shovels. It made for an idyllic scene. The Cape attracted so many families this time of year. Their presence always made Clairey feel a longing for the sense of familial acceptance she'd never experienced herself.

Tessa pulled her out of her melancholy thoughts. "Aren't you excited about the prospect of living in Manhattan for a few months?" she asked, taking a long sip of her water. "I've always loved New York City. Wouldn't mind living there."

"I've never really thought about it." Growing up right outside of Boston in the rough streets of Southie, she'd never really lacked for the experience of city life.

"I think you should do it," Tessa declared. "I don't know why you're even on the fence about it."

Truth be told, Clairey couldn't really explain her hesitation. Drexel really had handed her a chance to overcome the monumental setback of losing her job.

"Ask for more money, if that will make the decision easier," Tessa suggested.

Clairey toyed with the buckle on her bike helmet. "I can't justify doing that. The salary he offered was more than generous."

"Then, I don't really see why you're not jumping at the chance. You have no job. And not that I don't love having you there, but your primary residence is my pull-out sofa."

"It's my only residence. In my defense, I just haven't been able to find an affordable place yet. The Cape isn't exactly cheap this time of year, at the height of tourist season."

"All the more reason to say yes to this Drexel."

"There's a lot to consider, Tessa."

Tessa turned to stare at her for a couple of beats, then slapped a hand to her chest. "Oh, my! It's more than just surface attraction, isn't it?"

Clairey tried not to react to the truth in her friend's words. "I don't know what you're talking about."

"I think you do. You're genuinely drawn to him. You can't stop thinking about the man. And it's got you scared."

"That's ridiculous. I've had two whole conversations with him." But she'd lain awake all night unable to get the image of him out of her mind. Scenes replayed in her head of the way he'd looked at her when she'd barged into the conference room. The utter look of shock on his face when her plant had gone flying into him. The way he'd lovingly lifted his niece into his arms and wiped the pizza sauce off her face after their lunch.

"Me thinks doth protest a tad too much."

Clairey couldn't help her amusement. "You have just botched that line so marvelously. Shakespeare is sure to be rolling over in his crypt."

"Yeah, well, the overall idea still stands."

Clairey didn't have the words to deny what her friend was saying. Tessa was right. There was something about Drexel that had her unnerved about the way she reacted to him. He was the type of man that could have a woman head over heels before she knew it. Only problem with that was that he was way out of her league.

"Tell me more about him," Tessa directed. "You must have looked into him after he made his offer."

She had. She'd spent most of the night looking him up online right before she'd crawled into bed and then tossed and turned thinking about him nonstop. There were no shortages of write-ups about him on business sites.

"What did you find out?" Tessa prompted.

"Well, in addition to being handsome, he's wildly successful. He's in mergers and acquisitions. Started with a well-known international firm, then struck out on his own. He's also widely recognized for his near-genius instincts when it comes to investing. He's gone early into everything from popular websites to new tech

art-ups. Everything he's touched has grown
ponentially. He's Midas."

Tessa let out a low whistle. "Impressive."

Clairey left out the other details she'd read
out. The more gossipy sites that covered
rexel's private life. Every picture had him
le by side with a myriad of different beautiful
omen. He'd been snapped with everyone from
odels to actresses to Olympic-level athletes.

She had no idea how to fit into a life like that.

They sat silently, simply admiring the view
til Tessa jumped up and straddled her bike.
lairey followed her lead, and soon they were
ack on the bike path and pedaling at a steady
ace.

An hour later, after they'd circled back to
eir starting point, a voice-mail alert pinged,
d Clairey pulled her cell phone out of the bike
asket.

Drexel. Clairey's stomach did a little flip:
e had no idea what she might say when she
turned his call. Despite discussing little else
ith Tessa while they rode, she still had no idea
hat to tell him about his offer. Every time she'd
ecided and made up her mind one way or the
ther, a mountain of doubt emerged and stopped
er from following through with an answer.

She needed more time. She was about to call
nd tell him that when he beat her to it. Her
hone rang, and his contact number popped up

on her screen. May as well get it over with and tell him she had no answer for him just yet.

Clairey clicked on the call without giving herself a chance to hesitate.

"I'm not calling to pressure you," he said over the phone before she could so much as get a word out. "But I could use your help with something else."

Okay. Drexel's voice was tense and anxious. He sounded like a man at his wit's end. What was this about, then?

"Hello to you too."

She heard him utter a low curse. "I'm sorry. It's just that I have a very bored and confused little girl on my hands. Her father left this morning on his honeymoon, and it's just the two of us."

"I see."

"So far, we're off to a rocky start here. I could really use some assistance, Clairey. I could really use you."

What a fool he'd been. Drex had actually thought that he could handle a little girl by himself for one or two days until Clairey came to her senses and accepted his offer. His plan was to keep upping the salary and increasing the benefits and incentives until he reached an offer no sane person would refuse. But they hadn't even made it past late morning with no less han three tantrums. Marnie wanted to know where her father was and why he hadn't taken her along. Apparently, no one had explained to the poor child that she wouldn't be accompanying the couple on their next journey.

"What have you tried so far?" Clairey was asking him now.

"Everything from snacks to walks to attempts at a nap."

Clairey paused before answering. "She needs to be reassured that she's going to be all right. That you know what you're doing and you know how to take care of her."

Drexel grunted in frustration. "Well, that would be a bit of a fib, now, wouldn't it?"

"She just needs to believe it, Drexel."

The way she said his name, softly and with a clear note of respect, registered in his heart. Damn, she sounded sexy over the phone. And wasn't this a fine time to be thinking such a thing?

"I'll try my best."

"She also needs a distraction. Something to occupy her mind. She can't just sit there and busy herself while you try to get some work done."

Huh. That's exactly what he'd been doing. How in the world had she figured him out in such a short span of time?

"What do you suggest?"

"Marnie mentioned several times in cla.
how much she loves the water. Maybe take he
swimming."

He shook his head even though she couldr
see it. "No go. I asked if she wanted to hea
down to the pool. She said she hates the way th
other kids splash around in there and get her a
wet." His niece was upset about the prospect
getting wet. In a pool. Heaven help him, wh
world had he woken up in?

"I think she meant the ocean."

He hadn't thought of that. "Oh." Striding t
the window, he took a peek outside to the A
lantic a few acres away. "The beach, huh? I'v
never taken a little girl to the beach before.
looks pretty windy out there. The waves aren
exactly smooth."

"Do you know if she has floaties?"

"Is that some kind of kids' cereal or some
thing?"

He could practically hear her chuckling a
him. "No. Safety floaties. They're meant to kee
kids safely afloat in the water. She really shoul
have a set."

"If she does, I have no idea where they are.

"You can get them almost anywhere. Even th
grocery stores on the Cape carry them."

When was the last time he'd stepped foot i
a grocery store? He couldn't even recall.

Clairey was saying something else. "There'

a small, secluded area of beach off Old Silver. Only the locals know about it. It would be the perfect spot to take Marnie. I can send directions to your phone."

He rubbed his forehead. He was a grown man who'd been wildly successful in his area of business and had taken on more than his share of bullies, both in the corporate and the real worlds. But the prospect of spending the day alone on the beach with a five-year-old made his blood run cold with fear. "Listen, Clairey. Half a minute ago I didn't realize kids needed floaters or that they even existed."

"Floaties," she corrected.

"Right. My point is, this all sounds rather daunting. I'm ready to yield to you half my worldly possessions if you'll just come with us." He was only partially joking.

She paused long enough that Drexel had a moment of sheer panic. He was not above pleading with her if that's what it would take. "I'm willing to pay you for your time."

Several more moments of silence passed with Drexel holding his breath. Finally, he heard her heavy sigh over the tiny speaker. "That won't be necessary. I'll meet you at the location I'm about to send you. And I'll pick up the floaties that work best on my way there."

Drexel felt the tension loosen its grip on his

shoulders. "You are an angel sent from Heaven above."

Her only reply was to say she'd see him in about half an hour.

Drexel hung up the phone just as Marnie let out another shriek of frustration, this time because her cartoon had just ended on TV.

How in the world was he supposed to do this? Especially if Clairey turned down his offer? The very idea sent a shudder through his entire being. He had no idea how to raise a young girl. All his success in the business world meant naught in this particular situation. He could provide for a child, sure. But that was about it. As for the rest, Drex was absolutely clueless.

Nevertheless, he had to appreciate the small victory. The immediate crisis was averted. For now.

Releasing a long sigh of relief that the tantrums would be over soon, he flopped onto the bed and rubbed his weary eyes. He'd known Clairey would know what to do. Thank the heavens above he'd been right.

Over the phone he'd referred to Clairey as an *angel*. But the way she looked in a tankini top and swim shorts was downright sinful. He forced himself to look away and focus on the task at hand, setting up the large beach umbrella that Clairey had thought to bring.

"It never even occurred to me we'd need a sun umbrella," he admitted. "Thank you for think-ing of it." He had so much to thank her for, he didn't even know where to begin.

"Us locals know what's needed on a beach trip."

That was sure true. She'd thought of every-thing really. Whereas he'd simply grabbed sun-screen, a towel, and Marnie's sun hat, Clairey had brought a canvas beach bag loaded with ev-erything from juice boxes and snacks to sand toys.

Marnie clapped her hands in delight when they pulled out the latter. Clairey gave the girl a wide smile. "Are you ready for a fun beach day?"

Marnie squealed in delight before answer-ing, "Yeah!"

Satisfied that he'd dug the umbrella post deep enough that it wouldn't lift off in the oceanside wind, Drex finally allowed himself a calming breath.

But now Clairey was putting her hair up in a twist and then rubbing sun lotion on her shoul-ders, and he had to remind himself to keep breathing. Her dark wavy hair complemented her golden tanned skin. Her cat-eye sunglasses lent her a bohemian look. Dear Lord, was that a small tattoo over her hip bone? Drexel had never considered himself a fan of body art, but the tiny rendering of a star and moon that peeked out from the waistband of her shorts made him think thoughts he had no business entertaining. Not about the woman he hoped to hire as a temporary nanny.

Luckily, Marnie drew his attention before he got caught gawking. She pointed to the ocean waves. "Water!"

Clairey laughed and tapped the little girl's nose. "Yep. That's water, all right. Would you like to swim first or dig in the sand?"

Marnie seemed really torn about the decision. Finally, she reached for the bucket and shovel. In no time, she was knee-deep in sand.

Drexel tore his gaze away from his niece to stare at the woman who'd helped to turn his disastrous day around. She really made quite the picture stretched out on one of the towels she'd laid down for them. Her bathing suit was modest by most standards, but she looked more sexy and enticing than he wanted to acknowledge.

Without warning, she looked up to catch him staring at her. Drexel made sure not to squirm under her gaze.

"What?" she asked.

He did his best to look innocent. "Nothing. I'm just not one to sit idly on a towel, that's all. What does one do exactly on a so-called beach day?"

She chuckled and looked out over the water. "Precisely what we're doing."

"Making small talk?"

"Relaxing. Enjoying the ocean air. The sunshine." She flashed him a wide smile. "Aren't you enjoying all that? I am."

He was certainly enjoying her company. That he couldn't deny. But she was only here because he'd asked. "Listen, Clairey. I realize we've taken you away for the day. It's only fair you're compensated for your time."

"Compensated?"

He nodded. "I'll pay you for the hours you're spending with us."

She shook her head. "Oh, I won't accept your money. That's not what this is about."

What in the world? "I don't understand."

She shrugged. "Simple. I'd like my payment in the form of a dare."

A mischievous glint appeared in her eyes, and took all he had not to reach for her the way he so badly wanted to.

All right. He'd play along. "What kind of dare are we talking about here?"

"Do you like ice cream?"

At no point in this conversation would he have guessed that would be her next question. "I don't particularly go out of my way for it. But don't dislike it. Why?" What was she getting

at? Whatever it was, the playfulness in her voic
was amusing him to no end.

"There's an ice cream I'd like to see you try

He had to laugh at her. "If you want ic
cream, you can just say so, Clairey."

"This would be for you. But I get to pick th
flavor."

This sounded like it could be ominous fc
him. "And what flavor would that be?"

"There's a sweet shop in the center of towr
They have the best chocolate and the best ic
cream. And they're the only place I know tha
serves lobster vanilla caramel."

She couldn't mean real lobster. "You mea
candy, right? Gummy lobster of some sort?"

She shook her head. "Nope. Not candy. Rea
Maine lobster pieces served up in a cone of va
nilla with drops of hardened caramel."

Drexel felt his stomach roil in offense. "You'r
kidding. That flavor actually exists? And you'
like me to eat it?"

She nodded with clear humor. "You said yo
owed me for today, right?"

That was neither here nor there. "That's a rea
flavor? You're not just pulling my leg?"

She batted her eyes in mock innocence
"Would I ever do something like that?"

"And that's the payment you're asking fo
joining us today? That I try this atrocity of gas
tronomical insult?"

She chuckled, a soft delicate sound that seemed to hover in the air. "It's a delicacy. Tourists from all over the world visit that shop just to try it."

Drexel grimaced at the thought. "Are you sure can't just give you half my worldly possessions? Like I mentioned on the phone?"

She shook her head. "Nope. My terms are my terms. You eat the lobster ice cream. The whole cone. And I'll consider us squared."

He rubbed a hand through the stubble at his jaw. Of course he was going to take her up on her silly dare. But he wasn't going to acquiesce so easily.

"What do you say?" she asked. "Do we have a deal?"

"Fine," he finally said after making her wait several more moments. "I'll eat this affront to gastric sensibilities. If it will make you happy." He held out his hand for her to shake on the strange barter. Even though what he really wanted to do was pull her in his arms and kiss her senseless.

Half an hour later they were strolling through the center of town. Clairey had been there countless times, but today she seemed to be seeing it with fresh eyes. Maybe it was due to Marnie's influence. She was enthusiastically running into every tourist-trap gift store and

making her uncle buy countless worthless bau
bles that would no doubt end up in the garbag
can within a month's time. Or maybe it wa
being here with a charismatic and tall, dark an
handsome man who seemed to make both ma
and female heads turn. Clairey had thrown on
sundress over her beachwear, then helped Ma
nie get herself dressed in a dry top and fres
pair of shorts. As for Drexel—well, all she coul
think was that no one should look that appea
ing in a pair of swim shorts and casual loos
T-shirt. His dark olive skin was just sun-kisse
enough. And the shirt did nothing to conceal th
muscles of his chiseled chest. The watch adorr
ing his wrist further accented the pure mascu
line look of him.

As busy as he was, the man obviously worke
out regularly. She wondered if he did any pau
ticular sport. He certainly seemed athletic.

Stop.

Marnie grabbed her hand just then an
dragged her into yet another shop, this one muc
higher-end than the others. A clothing boutiqu
that sold designer women's clothing and hand
crafted purses, as well as other fairly price
items. Pricey enough that Clairey had onl
stepped foot in the place once, before walkin
back out within minutes. The little girl pulle
her over to a glass display case full of jewelr
made from rare colors of sea glass.

"Pretty," Marnie announced, her nose pressed up against the case.

"Yes, they are," Clairey agreed. "Very pretty."

Marnie looked up at her uncle. "Can I get that? Please?" She pointed to a choker necklace set atop a mound of cream-colored satin fabric. The kid had taste.

Without hesitation, Drexel turned to the saleslady who had come to stand next to them. "We'll take that necklace as well as the one next to it."

"Of course," the woman answered with a dazzling smile aimed only in his direction. "May I put it in a velvet box for you? It's only a small additional charge."

Drexel nodded.

Marnie hugged her uncle around the knees when the woman walked away. "Thank you!"

"You're welcome," he said, tousling her hair with affection.

Clairey couldn't help but feel touched by the scene. Sure, such an expense might be somewhat extravagant for a little girl. But the pieces would be something Marnie would treasure forever, along with the memory of how she came to acquire them. During such a time of confusion and upheaval for his niece, she didn't think it was unreasonable of Drexel to make such a purchase.

Despite Marnie's rather tumultuous young

life so far, the little girl had certainly lucked out in the uncle department.

The saleslady was back within moments with a decorated paper bag that she handed to Drexel. She still hadn't so much as looked in Clairey's direction.

Upon leaving the store, Clairey stopped dramatically and slapped her hands on her hips in mock seriousness. "Enough stalling. The sweet shop is two doors down."

Drexel tilted his head in resignation and held out his hand. "Lead the way."

Clairey walked them to the store and ordered strawberry for Marnie, at her request, mocha chocolate chip for herself, and the dreaded lobster vanilla caramel for Drexel.

She handed his cone to Drex with a somewhat naughty wink. Who was this unfamiliar woman? She hardly recognized herself, teasing a man she barely knew in such a manner.

He eyed the cone with an exaggerated shudder. "I have to eat the whole thing, huh?"

Of course, she wasn't going to make him if he really didn't want to. But she wasn't going to tell him that just yet. And so far, Drexel was being a good sport about the whole thing. Besides, everyone she'd seen have it for the first time was pleasantly surprised, herself included.

She watched as he took the first bite. His lips

tightened into a firm line. Then his eyes grew wide. "Huh! It's not half bad."

She couldn't help her chuckle. "You see? Sometimes it pays to try new things."

He took another, larger bite. "I guess you're right. I don't know if I'd order it again, but I'm not sorry I tried it."

"Right. Now you can say you've had a dessert that contained a crustacean."

Marnie held her ice cream up without a word and rubbed her eyes with clear exhaustion. She was too tired to even finish her cone.

Drexel lifted her up with his free arm, and she immediately tucked her head on his shoulder. "I think our girl's battery is running low. We should probably start heading back."

She had to force herself not to react to his use of the word *our*. It was just a figure of speech. He didn't mean anything by it. Certainly, he wasn't inferring anything that might mean the three of them were any kind of unit.

"She has done a lot today."

"I'll drive you back to your car."

When they made it back to the beach where they'd left his rental—a sporty convertible that had probably cost her whole month's salary to rent for the week—Clairey settled Marnie in her booster and buckled her in. The child then promptly fell asleep before Clairey had even clipped on her own seat belt. Drexel pulled out and started driving out of the parking lot.

Looking at the girl sleeping soundly in the back seat, Clairey had to come clean to herself.

There was nothing for it. Clairey couldn't deny how much she'd enjoyed herself today. Spending the day with Drexel and Marnie had comprised some of the most enjoyable hours she could remember in a long while. In fact, she couldn't recall a time she'd so thoroughly felt joy. Certainly not after she'd been so unceremoniously forced out of her home by her mother. Not that the days she'd lived in that house before her banishment could be described as anything resembling happiness.

On top of it all, Drexel had needed her today. He and Marnie both had.

It was a heady feeling, and she knew she had to tread carefully. No one had actually needed her before. Not really.

How in the world could she turn her back on that? She couldn't. She had to help Drexel get settled back in New York with a little girl in tow, and she had to help Marnie get adjusted to her new life. Clairey would accept his job offer, but she'd do it on her terms. Drexel needed to know that she only planned to take this job as a temporary assignment.

She turned in her seat to tell him before she could change her mind. "I'll do it," she blurted

without giving herself a chance to think any
more on it. "I'll take your offer to be your nanny
for Marnie."

Drexel's eyes grew wide, and a smile appeared on his lips. "You will?"

She could only nod. Then, before she knew it,
his arm was around her shoulders and his mouth
was on hers. Heaven help her, every inch of her
body responded, and she returned the spontaneous kiss.

CHAPTER FIVE

How in the world had she ended up here?
Clairey stared at the early-evening Manhattan
skyline as it slowly began to illuminate and
come to life. Five short days ago, she'd been
tossed out of a job with barely enough money
in her bank account for a sandwich.

Now, here she was. In a penthouse apartment
in New York's Upper East Side, overlooking
Central Park. A hefty advance had been de-
posited into her bank account. And she no longer had to sleep on her friend's couch at night.
Drexel's spare bedroom he'd had her move into
was the size of Tessa's whole apartment. All in
all, some pretty life-altering developments.

The only problem was she couldn't seem to
help but develop feelings for the man responsible for it all.

She felt his presence behind her before he
began to speak. "Are you settling in okay? Anything you need?"

She forced a casual smile on her face and

urned to face him. "Quite well, thank you." So
ar, they were doing a jolly good impression of
playing the ultimate professional duo of boss
nd employee.

If that kiss they'd shared in the parking lot
a few days ago entered Drexel's mind, he sure
wasn't showing any indication of it. While she
couldn't get it out of her mind.

Though, she really had to. Clearly, it had
meant nothing. Just a spontaneous, knee-jerk
reaction he'd had in a moment of relief that she'd
be taking the job. She had no business reliving
the sensation of having his lips on hers from
the moment she woke up in the morning until
she closed her eyes at night. And pretty much
every moment in between.

But Drexel obviously had forgotten about the
whole thing. A sharp pang of disappointment
ran through her chest before she swatted it away.

"Did you have enough dinner?" he asked her,
courteous beyond need. "Sharon's gone home
for the evening, but there are plenty of leftovers
n the fridge."

"Oh, no. I'm quite full. Sharon is a genius in
the kitchen. Dinner was delicious."

"Good. That's good."

Why in the world were things so awkward
between them now? Such a far cry from that
day back on the Cape when she'd made him try
lobster ice cream.

"Marnie seems to be settled in, as well," s
added, just for something to say. He knew ve
well how Marnie was doing. He'd seen to
himself that the girl had everything she neede

He nodded once. "I just checked on her. She
setting up the new dollhouse. I told her she cou
do that for an hour or two. Then she has to g
to bed."

For someone who had no experience wi
kids, the man sure seemed to be getting th
hang of having one around. He was a natura
"I'll go read to her in a bit and tuck her in. W
you be stopping by to say good-night to h
later?"

"I've already said good-night. I'll be headi
out for the evening."

It was then that she noticed what he wor
With him standing somewhat in a darkene
corner of the room, she hadn't realized befo
just how formal his attire was. A crisp whi
shirt and tailored black trousers appeared to l
the pieces of a tuxedo with the jacket yet to l
added. Along with gold cuff links that had prol
ably cost a fortune.

No doubt his plans for the evening involve
a glamorous night out with an equally glamo
ous woman who'd probably been waiting wit
bated breath for him to return to the city.

The disappointment she'd felt earlier turne
to a throbbing, searing ache. This was why she

hesitated in coming here. She had no business feeling as wounded as she did simply because he'd be spending the evening with another woman. What of it? It really was none of her business whatsoever. Despite the gnawing ache in the pit of her stomach.

Dear heavens. She was developing real feelings here. Feelings she had no right to. But who could blame her? Drexel Osoman was a prize by any standard. Not just because of his looks. Or his wealth. That was all surface level, as far as Clairey was concerned. No, it was more the way he behaved around his niece. Or how he made sure Clairey had everything she needed to settle into her new surroundings. He was attentive and considerate and a truly loving uncle. How was Clairey supposed to guard her heart around all that?

But the truth was she had no claim to him at all. Their arrangement was nothing more than a business one. She had to get that through her head and learn to live with it.

Maybe if she repeated it to herself over and over, it would gradually sink in.

"I hope you have a lovely time," she told him with a lightness she didn't feel.

He should never have kissed her. Hell, he should never have so much as touched her. Drexel bit out a curse as he strode down the hallway to grab his jacket and take the private elevator down to the waiting car in the street.

Things were so awkward and tense between them now. Gone was the easy and light camaraderie they'd shared the other day back on the Cape. So much so that he hadn't even been able to give her the necklace he'd gotten for her at that small boutique before they'd gone for ice cream. It still sat in its gift box on top of his dresser.

It would be much too awkward to give it to her now.

He half hoped she'd just come out and ask for it. She had to know he'd gotten it for her. Why did she think he'd bought two, for Pete's sake?

Well, he didn't have time to ponder any of it right now. He'd been unable to get out of the charity dinner he'd signed up for weeks ago. As much as he'd rather stay home and tuck Marnie into bed and then perhaps share a conversation with their newly hired nanny, he had to attend this shindig. Tara, his office administrator, had informed him in no uncertain terms when he'd offered to make a sizable donation instead of going, that it didn't work that way and that it wouldn't do to not make an appearance and afford the charity the type of publicity only a young billionaire could provide. He'd do his best to make it a quick night. Drexel would make an appearance, then he'd make his exit.

Would Clairey be waiting up for him when he returned?

Snap out of it.

He gave his head a quick shake and chastised himself for the thought. He had no business thinking of her that way.

There was only one reason Clairey was here at his penthouse, and that was to help Drexel with his niece. Heaven knew he needed her assistance. On top of running a demanding international business, making sure his mother had the best care, and dealing with all the other pressures on him, he was absolutely in over his head. Clairey was an absolute blessing—and one perfect for the role. After all, she'd stuck her neck out for Marnie before she'd even really known her.

But he couldn't forget her true purpose in their lives.

She wasn't there as his companion to greet him with a cup of tea or a glass of wine after he'd suffered through a boring night of speeches and fake haggling over bids.

There was no denying, however, just how much that image appealed to him. Then his imagination took it a step further. He pictured what she might be wearing at that time of the late evening as she joined him in a nightcap. Perhaps a well-fitting silk shirt she liked to sleep in with matching shorts that showed off her shapely figure. Maybe a revealing negligee.

Drexel sucked in a breath and swore yet again. Not quite under his breath and just as the elevator doors slipped open on the ground floor. The attendant at lobby desk gave him a startled look.

"Rough day, Mr. Osoman?" the man asked with a slight smile.

"Something like that," Drex answered as he made his way out to the waiting car.

His evening wasn't going to be any less rough, for that matter. Not if he couldn't stop thinking about one dark-haired and beguiling temptress who just happened to be sleeping in his apartment. And she would be for the foreseeable future. So he had to get over this fixation on her that he seemed to be developing, whatever it was.

He settled into the back seat and greeted his driver. Sure enough, within a block, his thoughts turned back to Clairey. Was she still reading to his niece? Or had she tucked the little girl in already? Maybe she'd crawled into bed herself right after. The image of her under satin sheets sprawled on the mattress invaded his mind.

Get a grip!

He had to stop these wayward thoughts once and for all. As far as he was concerned, he couldn't view Clairey any differently than Sha-

n, his housekeeper. They were both in his em-
loy and had to be considered the exact same
ay.

He grunted a laugh at that, earning him a
deways glance from his driver. Sharon was
grandmother of seven cut right out of central
asting if anyone needed a matronly type. And
lairey was about as far from matronly as *A*
as to *Z* in the alphabet.

"Just confirming we're not picking up any-
ne else, correct, sir?" Tom asked, breaking into
is thoughts.

"Correct."

He hadn't had a chance to ask Charlotte or
nyone else to accompany him tonight before
aving for the Cape for his brother's wedding.
nd he hadn't the inclination to call and ask
ny of his past dates once he'd arrived. He had
) wonder if that was due to a certain resort
mployee he'd met his first morning there. Too
ad he couldn't have brought Clairey along. She
ight have enjoyed the pageantry of it all. The
ver-the-top decorations and extravagant cana-
és. But of course, that would have been inap-
ropriate.

Wouldn't it?

Nothing said they couldn't attend events
uch as auctions together simply as friends. He
ubbed his forehead and stared out the window

at the passing scenery of the city. That was wish
ful thinking. Not to mention a slippery slope.

He couldn't risk getting close to Clairey i
any way. For one thing, she deserved much mor
than he had to offer. The men in his famil
didn't exactly have a stellar track record as fa
as stable, loving relationships were concerned
He had several projects at work he couldn'
allow himself to be distracted from. Oh, an
there was that whole new development wher
he was suddenly sole guardian of a little gir
It wouldn't be fair to date any woman with s
much on his plate, let alone a woman as dy
namic as Clairey.

No. She deserved much better than the like
of him.

There was someone else in the apartment
Clairey awoke with a start at the sounds com
ing from down the hallway. A glance at the digi
tal clock on her bedside table told her it wasn'
particularly late. Way too early for Drexel to b
back already.

She'd been so tired she'd crawled into bed
with a paperback bestseller right after tuck
ing Marnie in. She must have drifted off. Th
sounds coming from outside her room had
woken her up.

Maybe Marnie had woken up and was shuf
fling around. That could be dangerous. Half

sleep, the girl might not know her way around
ne penthouse at all. Clairey had turned off all
ne lights. Alarm shot through her at the thought
f Marnie moving around in the dark in an un-
amiliar apartment. She bolted out of bed and
lung the door of her bedroom open, flying to-
vard the kitchen area.

The sight that greeted her when she got there
alted her in her tracks. Drexel with his jacket
ff, his shirt sleeves rolled up, and the front of
is shirt unbuttoned halfway down his chest.
o ruggedly handsome, for a moment she for-
ot to breathe.

He looked up in the process of pulling a cov-
red dish out of the refrigerator, appearing as
hocked to see her as she was to find him there.

"Drexel? What are you doing here?"

He shrugged. "Just got back, came looking
or those leftovers I mentioned earlier."

Was he deliberately being obtuse? "I mean,
vhy are you here? In the penthouse?"

The corners of his mouth lifted. "I live here.
Remember?" He looked her up and down, and
current of heat arose as his eyes traveled over
er body. "Are you sleepwalking or something?"

She threw her hands up in frustration. "You
now what I mean. I wasn't expecting you back
o early." His date must have not gone well. Not
hat it was any of her business. Absolutely no
eason for her to feel any sense of relief mixed

with a strange headiness. "I'll leave you to
then," she added to spare herself the risk
gawking at him. The man sure looked good
an unbuttoned tuxedo shirt.

He stopped her before she'd gone more tha
three steps. "Do you like kittens?"

Maybe she was sleepwalking. Because h
question made absolutely no sense. "I'm sorr
Did you just ask me about kittens?"

He nodded. "Do you like them?"

What kind of person didn't like kittens? A
why in the world was he asking? "Yes. I li
kittens. They're very cute. Why do you ask?"

He set the plate he'd been holding down
the counter and shoved his fingers through h
hair. "I thought maybe Marnie would like a p
To help her adjust to moving in with me. I nev
had one growing up. I figured a kitten might
easier than a puppy in a high-rise."

Something tugged in her chest right arou
the vicinity of her heart. Drexel had obvious
been giving this some thought. He really want
to do right by his niece. Maybe Chase had dor
his daughter a tremendous favor in leaving h
to his brother to raise. Harsh as that sounded,
certainly hadn't been there for his child whe
she'd needed him the most. He'd practical
abandoned her. Whereas Drexel was doing e
erything he could to make sure Marnie was a
right.

Kittens! Drex certainly wasn't making it easy on her to ignore her growing attraction.

She went and stood across the kitchen island from him. "I think that's a wonderful idea."

The smile he sent her way nearly had her swooning. "You said that first day I had her that kids needed distractions," he reminded her. "What better distraction than a playful little cat?"

"I can't think of anything. I can call around to see about finding one. I'll start with nearby rescue shelters."

"You would do that for me?" he asked. "I mean, you'd do that for us? It doesn't exactly fall within the job description."

She nodded. "Then, consider it a friendly favor."

His lips grew thin, and something she couldn't name flashed behind his eyes. "Is that what we are? Friends?"

Clairey's heart skipped a beat. It was such a loaded question. Somehow, they'd gone from speaking about cute little kittens to discussing the defining parameters of their relationship.

"I'd like to think so," she answered as honestly as she could. Though, it wasn't one hundred percent honest because deep down she knew she wished for more.

"Then, I could have asked you to come with me tonight. As a friend."

"On your date?" she blurted out without thinking.

He blinked at her. "What?"

It occurred to her that she really had no idea exactly where he'd been or who he'd been with. "I just assumed... I mean, the way you were dressed. So formally. And you've been out of town." Oh, for goodness' sake, now she was just blabbering.

"What made you think I was out on a date?"

"I just assumed you probably had someone waiting for you while you were off on the Cape for your brother's wedding."

"Did it occur to you that there was a reason I was sans one at the wedding?"

Of course it had. But she wasn't about to admit it. "I hadn't given it much thought."

Liar.

His lips quirked into a small smile, and he looked at her as if he might be thinking the same thing.

"I'm not dating anyone right now," he announced, taking a bite of a sandwich he'd efficiently put together during their conversation. "I have too much happening at the moment."

She would have thought men like him always had time for romantic relationships. Someone with all the qualities Drex had wouldn't have to put too much effort in. "Oh?"

He nodded, took another bite, chewed and

swallowed. "My life was crazy enough with some major work projects coming due. Now I have to adapt to becoming a fill-in parent all of a sudden."

He slowly put the sandwich down on a plate and wiped his hands, as if he'd suddenly lost his appetite.

For the life of her, Clairey couldn't come up with anything to say to try to reassure him. The turn his life had unexpectedly taken really was rather daunting. His words rang in her head. He didn't have time for any kind of relationship. Not that she'd thought she ever had any kind of chance with him, but here he was making it quite clear. He didn't want to be romantically involved with anyone. Certainly not the woman he only saw as a caretaker to his niece. She had to squelch the disappointment that swelled in her chest.

After several silent moments, he snapped his head back up to look at her. "I asked you earlier if you liked kittens. Do you happen to like fireworks, as well?"

She had to chuckle at the sudden change of topic. "Yes. I like kittens, puppies and fireworks. Though, one of those things just doesn't belong here." The last phrase she sang to the tune of the well-known children's song that accompanied the matching game played in nursery school.

He crooked a finger in her direction. "Come here. I want to show you something."

Clairey stood off the stool and followed him as he walked down the hallway to the main living area. Where could he possibly be leading her after speaking of fireworks? She'd never met anyone like Drexel Osoman. Every moment was an unexpected adventure of some sort. "Kittens and fireworks. Sounds rather magical." And exciting, she added silently.

Just like the man himself.

The conversation was getting too loaded back there. He'd been too tempted to pour his soul out to her. And that just wouldn't do. Drexel knew what parts of his life he needed to keep guarded. For his own sake as much as for Clairey's. No need to burden her with the darkness that was his past.

So he'd thought of a distraction. He led her to the living area with its walls of glass that offered a sweeping panoramic scene of the Manhattan skyline. It was beautiful enough this time of night with the lights of the skyscrapers glowing brightly all around. As well as the brightly lit Brooklyn Bridge in the distance.

But tonight there'd be even more. The show should start in a matter of minutes.

"This view takes my breath away," Clairey said next to him as they took in the night.

"There'll be more to enjoy in a bit."

As he said the last word, a distant bouquet of ht bloomed in the sky to the west. He pointed at way. "Did you see that?"

Clairey's mouth fell open. "Well, I'll be darned. reworks? The Fourth was two weeks ago."

He nodded. "It was rainy in New York. The y itself never cancels, rain or shine. But a few the boroughs postponed to tonight."

"And we have a perfect view."

He pulled the love seat around to face the ndow, motioning for her to sit. "I say we enjoy e show. Would you like a glass of wine?"

She hesitated. "I really shouldn't. I have no ea how early Marnie will wake up tomorrow."

"Your choice. But I checked on her when I t in, and she was out like a light. I'm guess- g she'll probably sleep in. She's had a rather rrowing and exhausting few days."

"You think so?"

"I do. If not, I have some really strong Ja- aican Blue Mountain blend I always keep on nd."

"Sounds strong." She gave him a reluctant ile. "Maybe just one glass, then."

He walked over to the bar to open one of the rrel-aged merlots a client in Napa Valley had fted him. He didn't know a thing about her ine tastes or coffee tastes, or anything else she und pleasurable, for that matter.

He had to suck in a breath. Bad direction fc his thoughts to have taken.

Nevertheless, the merlot was sure to please He'd bet on it.

Clairey had settled on the love seat with he legs tucked under when he handed her the glas of wine.

She didn't tear her eyes away from the win dow. By this point, another set of firework could be seen in the distance, this one cleare and a bit closer in the sky.

She took a small sip of her wine, and her eye grew wide. "This is really good."

He'd been right. A rush of pleasure surge through his chest. He liked pleasing her. "I'n glad you like it."

They sat in silence for the several minutes. I was over all too soon.

She set her half-empty wineglass on the floo by her feet. "That was lovely, Drexel. Thank yo for thinking to show me."

"I'm glad you liked it," he repeated. *Way t go, fella. Keep dazzling her with your witty con versation.*

"I really did. I had to work on the Fourth an missed the fireworks on the Cape. I'd actually been kind of sad about it. Before this job, I'c make sure to catch them in Boston. They have theirs over the harbor. I would take the T int the city with friends and spend the day in the commons until it grew dark and was time to head over to the Green Line."

She sounded wistful. He said, "Sounds fun. There's something about watching them in the sky over water. I've seen the ones in Atlantic City a couple of times."

"Oh?"

He nodded. "I grew up in New Jersey. Right outside of Hamilton."

"I've never been to Atlantic City. Or anywhere in Jersey for that matter."

"You haven't missed much. Atlantic City is a smaller version of Vegas. With a disproportionate slew of seedy areas." He cringed thinking about all the seediness he'd been exposed to in his life.

"But the casinos must be fun."

She was wrong there. Casinos weren't much fun if your dad happened to have an addiction to gambling. "I didn't particularly care for them. I still don't."

He wasn't about to get into the reasons for that opinion and wished he could forget them himself.

No, the days and nights Drexel had found himself in a casino had never been any fun. Far from it.

CHAPTER SIX

WAS IT SOMETHING she'd said?

Clairey watched as the muscles along Drexe[l]
jaw tightened. He stiffened where he sat on th[e]
love seat. Suddenly, their light and easy conve[r]
sation seemed anything but.

She grasped for something to say to get som[e]
semblance of it back. "There's something ve[ry]
unique about watching fireworks from a di[s]
tance like this, in a high-rise apartment. It fee[ls]
so…intimate somehow."

He sucked in a small breath. Wrong choic[e]
of words. One that could be taken in so man[y]
ways.

"I just mean it feels very private. The Fourt[h]
of July festivities I've gone to in Boston attra[ct]
thousands of people."

He shot her a warm smile. "Sounds fun."

"One of my favorite days of the year whe[n]
I was a kid. My dad would get us up early t[o]
take the T into the city." She laughed as th[e]
bittersweet memories stormed her mind. "Hon[e]

estly, he acted more excited than me. My mom just sort of tolerated the long day and night in the city. She isn't one for crowds. My dad and I, though, we both loved every minute of it. I still do."

"And what about your father now?"

A sharp stab of hurt. "I'm afraid I lost him years ago, around middle school." In a very real sense, she'd lost her mother then too. Never the very motherly type, Nora had become increasingly distant after the loss. Then she'd met Frank and had become a completely different person altogether.

"I'm very sorry to hear that. It must be very hard on you and your mother not to have him around any longer."

Her lips trembled. Dad's loss had hit her mother hard, but she'd gotten over it surprisingly quickly. "My mother has moved on. She remarried several years ago, and they moved out to Arizona. I hardly see her anymore." Or hear from her, for that matter, she added to herself.

"Again, I'm sorry," Drexel said on a soft whisper. He leaned her way, and for one crazy instant, she thought he might touch her. But he stood instead. "I could use some more wine," he announced, lifting his goblet, his fingers tight around the stem. "How about you?"

She shook her head. "Definitely not. Though, it's delicious, I must say."

Clairey watched as he poured from the bottle. He appeared uncomfortable, strained. Maybe she shouldn't have shared so much about her past with him. She'd clearly made him uncomfortable somehow.

He remained silent as he sat back down next to her, his gaze fixed on the distant night sky. Clairey didn't think he was even looking at the view anymore. He seemed lost in his own thoughts.

This was all so confusing. She had no idea how to communicate with this man. The parameters of their relationship still needed to be worked out. In a very real way, Clairey was the catalyst that had led to this drastic change in his life. Though, judging how quick Chase was to toss his daughter to her uncle, she suspected eventually the end result would have been the same. It had simply been a matter of time. If that meant that Clairey had somehow saved Marnie so much as a day of feeling unwanted and unloved, she would consider it a win. Marnie deserved to feel both those things. All children did.

All that aside, Drexel made her more than a little nervous. Still, for the life of her, she couldn't figure out what she'd said to cause yet another awkward silence.

Finally, she could stand the silence no longer. At the risk of overstepping her bounds, she forced herself to ask the question burning in her mind. "You seem to have drifted off somewhere. Feel like talking about it?"

When he slowly turned his head to face her, his eyes were clouded with clear pain.

"I'm sorry to be such poor company. It's just been…a lot, these past few days."

There was more to it, she knew. And now she'd gone and insulted him. "I didn't mean to imply you were being poor company. I don't expect you to entertain me, Drexel."

He tilted his head and saluted her with his wineglass. "I'm not used to seeing a friendly face after a long day."

She chuckled. "I'm not sure how friendly I could have looked. I wasn't expecting you and panicked at first, hearing noises."

"Still. Arriving home tonight felt rather different. In a good way. It was a pleasant experience not to walk into an empty apartment. Something I haven't really had the pleasure of too often in the past."

It was all she was going to get, no doubt. Nevertheless, a feeling of gratifying warmth spread inside her at his words.

He stopped her before she could set foot over the threshold with a gentle touch on her elbow. Gentle or not, she felt a current run through the tips of his fingers all the way through to her chest. "Just one more thing."

"Oh?"

"There's something that's been on my mind. Something I think we need to discuss."

Well, that sounded rather ominous. Had she done something wrong with Marnie? Great, barely a moment on the job, and she was being reprimanded already. "What is it?"

"The day I kissed you back there on the Cape, when you first accepted my job offer."

"Yes?"

"I've been meaning to apologize for that. I shouldn't have so much as touched you without asking."

Her mouth went dry. Dare she admit that she'd liked it? That far from having to be sorry, he'd given her a moment of pleasure she couldn't stop thinking about?

The courage escaped her. She gave a brisk shake of her head with a nonchalance she didn't feel. "It was nothing."

His lips tightened, and he nodded once. "Be that as it may, I offer my apologies." The way his moods seemed to switch from warm and giving all the way to ice-cold and formal was going to give her whiplash.

"I'll bid you good-night, then," he added.

Without another word, he turned on his heel and strode down the hall to his own suite. Clairey thought about calling after him to tell

im how much she enjoyed watching the fire-
orks but hesitated too long in her indecision.
Just as well.

omething about the woman made him act all
inds the fool.

It was nothing.

Her words echoed in his ears. He had no busi-
ess feeling disappointed that she'd referred to
heir kiss as if she'd already forgotten it had
ven happened. What a fool he was to have
rought it up again.

In his defense, when he'd arrived home, he
adn't expected a beautiful woman to come
unning out into the kitchen in sleep shorts and
loose-fitting T-shirt. An outfit that somehow
oked sexier on her than any negligee.

He bit back a curse. Great. Now he was think-
g of her in a negligee. Drex pounded the
illow under his head and tossed for the ump-
eenth time onto his other side. He'd crawled
to bed almost an hour ago and was still no-
vhere near falling asleep. His mind kept re-
laying the scene with Clairey earlier tonight.
he way she'd opened up to him about the loss
f her father. How he'd gone silent in response.
Discussions about the past, his past, made him
ncomfortable. He hadn't wanted to risk the tales turning and having his own past become
he topic of discussion.

She may have opened up to him, but Dre
wouldn't do the same in return. How would h
begin to explain the pressures that had been pu
upon him since he was barely more than a teen
Pressure to keep the family afloat, to keep foo
on the table, to pay the bills by working severa
manual-labor jobs and hiding his pay before hi
dad got ahold of it so that he could feed it to th
slot machines.

He cringed at the memories and forced then
away. If anything, the pressures had only grow
as he'd gotten older. Now, he had to make sur
his mother's care facility was paid for. He ha
to ensure Chase had a chance to reach his ful
potential. And now there was a little girl to sup
port.

All of the many reasons this deal with th
sheikh was so important.

No. Clairey couldn't understand, but Drexe
had made the right move in clamming up an
then walking away. It had taken almost all o
his will, but he'd made sure to maintain a dis
tance like a true professional would with some
one in his employ.

So why did it feel so wrong that this restles
insomnia plagued him now?

He didn't have an answer, and he didn't know
what to do about it. Those questions still both
ered him about six hours later when he finally
gave up and shoved the covers off. It was no

se. He was pretty much going to be shot for
ıe day, given his intermittent bouts of sleep.
Ie couldn't have gotten more than an hour or
o combined.

Not bothering to grab a shirt, he flung his
oor open with disgust and made his way out
o the kitchen…to find that now it was his turn
o be startled by Clairey the way he'd surprised
er last night.

She was already up and puttering around the
itchen. He didn't need to glance at his watch to
now it was barely past dawn. She'd changed into
oose-fitting gray sweatpants and a scarlet tank
op that fell just above her hips. Above the low-
vaisted sweatpants, it afforded him a glimpse of
alf an inch of skin and sent his blood shooting
ot through his veins.

When she noticed him, she stilled in the act
f pulling a pot out of one of the lower cabinets.

"You're up early," he said, stating the obvious.

She yawned in response before speaking.
Tell me about it. But I wanted to get a head
tart on Marnie's breakfast and begin planning
er day. I want everything to be smooth sailing
rom the start."

Huh. "That was smart. I'm sure she'll appre-
iate it." As did he. "Thank you."

She shrugged. "No need for thanks. Just
loing my job."

Drex didn't bother to tell her what he was

thinking. Not every nanny would wake u
at the crack of dawn to ensure the day we
smoothly for their charge. But he was gratef
for it. The fates had certainly smiled on both
them where Clairey was concerned. One of th
few things in his life he could say that about

The sadness he'd taken note of in her ey
last night still swam in their depths. It ma
him want to take her into his arms and hold h
tight against his chest to comfort her. He shou
never have brought up her parents last night.

"Look, I didn't mean to pick at old woun
last night, when I asked about your father. I'
sorry if our conversation made you sad in ar
way."

She gave her head a vehement shake. "Plea
don't apologize. I don't mind talking about hir
Of course it's sad that he's gone." Drexel did
miss the hitch in her voice and the slight pau
before she could continue. "And I miss him te
ribly, but his memory truly brings me comfoi
He really was a great man. A great dad."

"I'm glad one of us can say that about eith
parent." Drexel flinched as soon as the word
left his mouth. He hadn't meant to say that pa
out loud.

"I'm guessing you didn't get along with or
or both of your parents. Your father?"

Childish as it was, he made the motion o

a finger-gun in her direction. "Bingo. Second guess gets the prize."

She chewed the bottom of her lip, hesitated before continuing. "Drexel, I want you to know that I'm a really good listener. I'm all ears if you'd ever like to talk. Now or any other time."

There was nothing but sympathy in her eyes. Her facial expression flushed with concern and worry for him.

But all he could see was pity.

He felt every muscle in his body tighten. This was exactly what he'd been trying to avoid last night. Somehow, he'd walked straight into the same perilous territory mere hours later. Something about Clairey had him acting uncharacteristically unreserved and with his guard down all too often. It made him annoyed with himself. So he took it out on her.

"Look, I don't really have time to stand here and participate in any kind of deep conversation. I have an international call to make soon, and it's nonstop meetings and deliverables after that until late evening."

What a cowardly way to say he didn't want to talk about it.

She jammed her hands on her hips and blew out a puff of air. The first gesture of frustration he'd ever seen from her. He had to wonder if he'd pushed her too far.

Though he desperately wanted to take back

every harsh word, he knew he'd deliberately lashed out at her. In fact, it was better this way. This was good. Better she knew exactly what a son of a bastard he could be and not expect any better.

Doing so would only cause her hurt in the long run.

CHAPTER SEVEN

YET AGAIN WITH the emotional whiplash.

Clairey watched as Drexel poured himself some type of coffee from a complicated-looking machine on the counter near the fridge.

"Help yourself," he uttered to her before walking away to his suite of rooms.

Then she watched his retreating back, the rigid set of his shoulders, the stiffened spine. Clearly, he was having trouble adjusting to having people in his apartment. Despite what he'd said last night about coming home to a friendly face. Apparently, waking up to one was a different matter.

She huffed out a frustrated breath. That would teach her, wouldn't it? This wasn't exactly a piece of cake for her either. Clairey was the one who'd abruptly found herself in a new city and a new residence. Not to mention a job she barely had the experience for. She had some of her own adjusting to do.

Well, one thing was for certain. She'd learned

her lesson. She refused to put herself out there again where Drexel was concerned. No more personal conversations, no more friendly chats. From now on, she would be the utmost professional. Every discussion would center around Marnie or something that might affect her.

Clairey was done. With a capital *D*. From now on, her sole and only focus would be the five-year-old girl sleeping down the hall.

Now, what might said little girl like for breakfast?

Clairey certainly had options when it came to making that decision. Drexel's housekeeper had the pantry and fridge fully stocked. She'd been told the woman typically had Mondays off. It was all typed up neatly for Clairey on a long document that she'd pulled up on the laptop Drexel had provided in her room. Everything she'd need to know about what he may require of the nanny he'd hired. Laid out in very clear terms in digital pixels on a master file he'd entitled *Marnie Osoman*.

So very efficient of him.

Her ward woke up and entered the kitchen just as Clairey flipped the last pancake onto a serving platter. She'd also cut up some berries and poured a tall glass of milk.

"Perfect timing."

Marnie clapped her hands together. "Pancakes!" Pure delight rang in her voice.

"I remembered one morning back at the Sea ew. You were eating nothing but pancakes at breakfast buffet," she explained.

"I'm glad you remembered that."

Clairey helped her get settled on a counter ol and set up plates for them both.

"Where's Uncle Drex?" the little girl asked er taking several bites and downing half the lk. "Isn't he going to eat with us?"

"He's a little busy at the moment. I'm sure 'll see him later, though," Clairey answered. pefully, she wasn't lying.

Three hours later, she was starting to suspect e might have done just that. They'd already ent the morning coloring and working on her ters and over an hour playing with the intri- tely designed dollhouse in Marnie's room. e girl had asked about her uncle often enough nes that Clairey had lost count.

For Marnie's sake, she would venture into the overbial lion's den and ask if Drexel planned perhaps have lunch with the girl. Or even say imple hello.

His office door was slightly ajar, and he didn't pear to be on the phone. Drexel noticed her fore she could knock.

"Was there something you needed?" he asked, early distracted. Clairey figured it would seem ss intrusive if she just spoke to him from the llway.

"I understand your days are certain to b
busy. I just thought maybe you could brea
away, given it's her first full day here and all.

He shook his head. "I'm afraid I can't. An
it's not just days. I'm afraid my evenings an
weekends are pretty full as well. I have a lot o
international clients who expect me to be avai
able at all hours. When I'm not dealing wit
them directly, I'm prepping for the times I wi
be." He waited a beat, then added, "I also do
lot of traveling."

"I see." She swallowed, forced herself to con
tinue to say what she had to say.

"Don't you think that might be a problem?
mean, long-term?"

He blinked at her. "Problem? What kind o
problem?"

"Marnie's certain to get bored and tire of m
if I'm the only one she sees all day. Day afte
day."

"She'll be going to school in the fall."

"It's still mid-July. That's still several week
away."

"Fine. I'll make a call." He pivoted on his hee
and walked back to his desk before she coul
ask him what he was talking about.

A call? What kind of call would address th
fact that he'd ignored his niece all day?

She found out the answer to that question
fifteen minutes later when Drexel called he

nto his study. He was seated at his U-shaped
dark mahogany desk with four large monitors
facing him. He didn't bother to look up or stop
typing when she entered the room.

"You called for me?"

Drexel continued pounding on the keyboard
as he answered. "The lobby desk downstairs informed me that most of the families with small
children are at their summer residences until
school starts."

Now she understood. Enough to have her
heart sinking a little.

Drexel continued. "But there's a family on
the fourth floor with a daughter around Marnie's age who had to stay in the city, something
having to do with their house in the Hamptons
being renovated. I had the desk call to set up a
get-together between the girls. They should be
here after lunch."

"You set up a playdate."

He paused long enough to glance at her, eyebrows raised. "Is that what they call it? I suppose I did."

Clairey opened her mouth to explain that
wasn't exactly what she'd had in mind but
snapped it right back shut. What was the use?
He clearly wasn't going to tear himself away
from his study anytime soon. And this girl
would be here within a couple of hours. Plus,

Drexel looked rather pleased with himself.
see," she answered instead.

"Maybe they'll even stay for dinner."

"Dinner?"

"I'll be out. I have a dinner meeting in th
financial district. You should ask them if the
can join you and Marnie."

"I might do that."

"Get something delivered. Or you can
head out. I've provided a list of my favori
nearby restaurants."

"Yes, I know. It's all right there in the Ma
nie file on my computer."

He nodded once. "That's right."

Clairey tried to quash the feelings of disa
pointment that flushed through her. Was th
how things were going to be for her and Ma
nie? Finding ways to keep themselves busy wi
playdates and other distractions while Drex
spent all his days glued to his desk and all h
evenings out and about?

If that notion made her feel lonely, that wa
solely her problem. But this wasn't about he
The bigger concern was, of course, Marni
The girl needed another anchor in her life b
sides her nanny, for heaven's sake. Clairey ha
to somehow make Drexel see that. And she ha
to do it in a way that wasn't overstepping he
bounds. After all, Clairey couldn't stick arou
forever. This job was a temporary one: she ha

a career she'd studied and worked hard for. As much as she was growing to care for the little girl, Clairey being here wasn't meant to be a permanent solution.

Drexel had to know that, didn't he?

If he didn't, he was in for a rude awakening when the time came. Clairey would have to do everything she could to make sure little Marnie didn't bear the brunt of it.

When the door buzzer went off just after three o'clock, Clairey realized with no small amount of surprise that she was rather nervous. She'd never entertained anyone who was successful enough to live in a building such as this one.

Smoothing out her skirt and adjusting her ponytail, she went to answer. Her sigh of relief was audible after opening the door. She should have guessed. The woman standing there, holding the hand of a smiling girl, was about the same age as Clairey and wore black denim jeans and athletic sneakers, her auburn hair secured in a large clip. Clearly, this was a babysitter too.

"Please, come in."

The little girl bounced through the door ahead of her sitter and announced, "Hi, I'm Sara." Definitely not a shy one.

By contrast, Marnie was hovering hesitantly by Clairey's leg, chewing on her thumbnail.

"And I'm Lana," the young woman said with a smile, following her charge inside the apartment.

Clairey gestured toward Marnie and introduced her to the two newcomers. "Thank you so much for taking the time to meet us. And on such short notice too."

Lana clasped a hand to her chest. "Oh, thank you for thinking to contact us. It's been so boring around here for Sara with all her friends away for the summer. We're usually at the Hamptons this time of year, but the house is being renovated, and it's taking so much longer than they thought."

"I see. Well, how fortunate for us that you happened to have stuck around this season!"

"Thank you. What's keeping you from heading to your summer place, then?" Lana asked.

Now, there was something to consider. It occurred to her that Drexel probably had multiple other residences. As successful an investor as he was, his holdings had to include real estate. She would have to find a way to ask him about it.

Clairey motioned for them all to follow her inside to the sitting area. "Actually, I don't quite know where that might be or even if there is one. See, this is literally one of my first days on the job."

Lana's eyes lit up with interest. "Oh? What service are you with? This penthouse has been occupied for a while. How did we never know there was a little girl Sara's age living here?"

"It was a private arrangement," Clairey answered simply, avoiding the second part of Lana's question and hoping it would drop the subject. As innocuous as the question was, she didn't feel comfortable discussing Marnie's situation with strangers, friendly as they were.

Lana glanced around the apartment and walked over to the glass wall to look out at the skyline. The girls were already ankle-deep in coloring books around the center coffee table.

"Wow," the other woman said, taking in the view. "This place is even grander than I thought. What do your employers do, again?"

Drexel chose that moment to step out of his office. He'd unbuttoned the top two buttons below his collar and rolled up his sleeves. A slight layer of stubble had begun to appear on his chin. The man looked like he could have stepped out of a cologne ad. Lana must have thought so too. Her expression when she turned and saw him could best be described as awestruck.

He looked from Clairey to the two girls with crayons and coloring books strewn all around his floor, and for a brief second looked completely, utterly confused. Then clarity washed over his features. Clairey felt a pang of sympathy for the poor man. What a life change he was experiencing. Barely two weeks ago, he was living the life of a bachelor with no responsibility to anyone but himself. Now he was suddenly living with a woman and accommodating the needs of a small child.

"Hello," he said to the other babysitter. The girls hadn't even bothered to acknowledge him, too engrossed in their activity. He waved to Lana and introduced himself.

"I see the playdate is in full session," he remarked, waving a hand toward the girls.

"It is indeed."

"Good. That's good. Well done." Drexel excused himself to head to the kitchen.

Lana blew out a breath and uttered something that sounded like it might have been *hubba-hubba*.

She turned to Clairey, her eyes wide. "Oh, my... Is that who you work for?" She patted her hair. "Someone should have warned me. I would have at least put some makeup on. That man could tempt a mother superior with those looks."

Something twitched in the center of Clairey's chest. Something she refused to examine as any kind of jealousy.

Lana continued, "His wife must be something. What's she like?"

"There is no wife."

"Oh? Then, how—?"

Clairey cut off her question. She was not

bout to get into any of that with someone she'd
terally just met. Drexel deserved to have his
rivacy protected. She would discuss with him
t an opportune time how much he wanted to
veal to his neighbors about who Marnie was.

She deftly changed the subject. "It's a long
tory. I'm hoping this won't be our last visit
gether, and I can tell you all about it some-
me. But before I forget, I was wondering if you
ould help with something. Do you happen to
now where we might be able to get a kitten?"

Lana still stared in the direction of the
itchen. "I'm sorry. What'd you ask?"

"I asked if you knew where we might be able
 go about finding a kitten to adopt."

The other woman blinked with a small shake
f her head and finally turned her focus back
 Clairey.

"A kitten." She smiled wide. "You're in luck.
ly sister happens to work for a rescue in West-
hester. I can ask her, if you'd like?"

With the uncomfortable conversation about
larnie's past diverted for now, Clairey walked
ver to the couch and motioned for Lana to join
er. As soon as Drexel was done in the kitchen,
he'd go brew them some tea. In the meantime,
he would go about finding a pet for Marnie as
ey'd discussed last night.

She just might be getting the hang of this
annying thing.

* * *

Drex tiptoed carefully out of his office two
hours later in an effort to avoid running into
Marnie and Clairey's guests if they were still
there. Nothing against them personally, he just
wasn't any good at small talk. And he espe
cially didn't know what he might possibly say
to a sitter and her small charge. Hell, he barely
knew how to speak to the child he was now re
sponsible for.

The apartment was quiet: no giggling little
girls and no sound of grown-ups' voices chat
tering in friendly conversation. Looked like the
coast was clear. Except, as soon as Drexel had
that thought and took a few steps, a small blur
in a pink tutu shot toward him and hugged him
around the knees.

"Hey there, kiddo."

Clairey rounded the corner after his niece.

"Uncle Drex!" Marnie squealed with excite
ment. "I made a new friend. And she was so
nice, and she colored with me, then we played
dollhouse, and we had a snack. She was so
nice!" she repeated.

Clairey laughed softly. "Marnie had a lovely
visit with Sara."

"I can see that."

Marnie barely let him finish his sentence.
"Oh! And she told me about the other kids that
live here. She says they're so much fun to play

with too. They all go to the same school, and they say the teachers are really nice, and it has a great playground." The child paused just long enough to take a quick breath. "Sara says I have to go to that school too. Can I please? Please, Uncle Drex. Can I?"

Drexel crouched down to her level. "I don't see why not. We'll make sure you go to the same school all your new friends will be at."

Marnie hopped excitedly. "Yay! Thanks, Uncle Drex." She gave him a tight hug around the neck, and Drexel could swear he felt a slight loosening in the tightness that always seemed to be gripping his chest. He returned her hug. "You're welcome."

Marnie gave him another squeeze before unwrapping her arms. "I'm gonna go look at all the pictures we colored."

Drexel stood up to find Clairey staring at him. She was looking at him like he'd just slayed a dragon. For what? Returning his niece's hug? He was probably imagining it. "She seems very excited about going to this new school."

She nodded. "I'll call Sara's nanny to get the details. She gave me her contact info."

"Uh, thank you. That would be great."

Clairey pulled her cell phone out of her pocket. "In fact, I'll do it right now. No time like the present. Right?"

"I suppose."

Drexel waited while Clairey placed the ca
and asked about the school. Then he watche
as her smile faded.

"Oh. I see," Clairey said into her phone. Sh
looked like someone might have just deflate
her birthday balloon and beaten her to blowir
out the candles on her cake.

"Well, thank you for the information. I
relay it all," she added, then disconnected th
call.

"What did she say?" he asked, though he w
fairly certain he didn't want to know the a
swer. Clairey's words and her expression d
not bode well.

"As it turns out, that school is one of the mo
popular and esteemed ones in all of New York

"Isn't that a good thing?"

"Sure. In the sense that anyone who's planne
enough in advance to apply and interview for
coveted spot in one of their classes is guara
teed a great elementary education."

"Six weeks isn't enough advance to apply?

A sound escaped from her lips that could I
described as a combination of both scoff ar
chuckle. "I'm afraid not."

Drexel felt a surge of disappointment pun
mel his core. He hated to think about how Ma
nie would react to the disappointing news. He
practically promised her she'd be able to atter

this school with her new friend and the other building neighbors her age.

He rubbed his eyes. "All right. We'll make sure to explain to Marnie that she just has to wait until next year. And that we'll find her another school she'll like just as much. She might not even want to switch from whatever school she attends by then."

Clairey's lips tightened. "Well, that would indeed be a good thing. I'm afraid next year isn't going to work either, for the school in question."

"What? Why?"

Clairey pressed her fingers to her forehead. "Lana just told me that the wait list is long. Really long."

"How long would that be?"

She wrung her hands together. Yet another bad sign. "Drexel, parents apparently apply upon their kid's *birth*. They go through years of communication and a rigorous review process. I'm afraid there's no hope of getting Marnie into the Hammond School. Not based on what I just heard."

Great. Now he would have to break the news to his niece that would break a promise he'd made. He swore out loud. How could he have been so stupid as to reassure her of something he had no clue about? He didn't want to be yet another adult who'd let Marnie down. He should have been more careful with his words.

His mind flooded with all the times he'd been let down by a distracted and uncaring father. Promises broken. All the lies about finally changing his ways. Drex had sworn throughout his life never to behave that way himself. Especially not toward anyone he cared about. And here he was on the first few days with his niece about to break a pledge he'd made to her.

Clairey's next words somewhat helped to mitigate the storm of self-recrimination rushing through his core. "Except she did mention one thing. A small possibility we might still be able to get Marnie enrolled."

He stepped toward her. "What kind of possibility? Whatever it is, we have to try."

"Lana said she'd forward me all the info via email. But apparently the Hammond School holds an event every summer."

Drexel stifled the urge to groan out loud. He was already up to his ears in functions and charity events to appease one client or colleague or another. "What kind of event?"

"Apparently it's a huge gala of some sort. Centered around an auction to benefit their sister school in San Juan. The final event is a draw."

"A raffle?"

She nodded once. "Exactly. The buy-in is an exorbitant amount, from what I understand."

That wasn't surprising. "What's the prize?"

"A coveted spot for one lucky student who can afford the tuition at the Hammond."

Drexel ran a hand over his face. It was clear what he had to do. Anything he could to help Marnie transition into her new life and ease the hurt of having her father abandon her without any regard whatsoever.

"Tell me exactly what the email says," he directed Clairey. "If there's any way we can purchase a lottery ticket, let's do it ASAP. I don't want to risk them selling out or anything."

"Aye, aye," she responded, with a mock salute, just as her phone pinged with an alert of some kind. Clairey glanced down at her screen. "Huh. Looks like she's already sent the info. I'll go download the document on the computer."

He started to follow her to her room.

"I hate to ask," she said over her shoulder as they made their way down the hall. "Lana said the price was *exorbitant*. Her exact word."

He shrugged. "Doesn't matter. I'll pay whatever it costs."

At this point, the expense was inconsequential. He'd made what amounted to a promise to Marnie out there. He didn't want the start of their time together to begin with a broken one. Kids were resilient, he knew. Heaven knew he'd had to be, growing up. But they could become weary all too easily. He didn't want his niece to feel that way about him.

When they reached Clairey's room, he hesitated before stepping inside. These were her private quarters. But she made no move to stop him, so he went to stand beside her as she sat down at the French antique desk he'd had set up for her with a laptop. But not before he had a chance to notice how much she'd made the place her own. Several framed photographs of her and various friends smiled out at him from every corner of the room. A painted tapestry hung on the wall by the door.

No one in any of the pictures seemed much older than she was. She had no photos with her mom.

Before he could even register what it was, his gaze traveled to a wire rack sitting right by her bathroom door. Various delicate lingerie items were hanging on it. A silky, lacy number in scarlet red made his pulse quicken. For as strait-laced as she appeared, Clairey Robi's taste in undergarments ran toward the boudoir variety. No use for it: he couldn't help but imagine the way she'd look wearing it. The pleasure that would come from taking it off of her.

He had to swallow down the rush of desire coursing through his veins and yanked his eyes away. The last thing he needed was to be caught ogling his nanny's underwear.

In the file he'd prepared, he'd made sure to include the laundry service he used as well as

ere to find the washer and dryer. So why
dn't she used either, for heaven's sake? Now
would never be able to get the image of her
earing…*that* out of his head.

Taking a deep breath, he bent over the desk
xt to her and made himself focus on the laptop
reen as she clicked the mouse. She had several
ndows open. A few of the article titles caught
s eye: "Helping Your Elementary-aged Child
rive." "Reading-skill Levels for School-aged
ildren." "Ensuring Your Child Is Eating Right."
She'd been reading up on how to best take
re of Marnie.

First week or not, he was already thinking
out giving her a raise. The woman was clearly
dicated.

Loyal and affectionate. How many such
ople had Drex met throughout his life? Not
ough. Then again, Clairey was one in a mil-
n. Someone a man could easily find himself
lling for if he wasn't careful.

He would have to make sure he was careful.
Drexel found himself staring at her profile
she navigated the computer screen. She re-
ly was striking. Her dark hair brought out the
ight hue of her eyes. The mass of curls com-
emented her patrician nose and soft chin.

"Here," she said after a few moments and
inted at the screen. "The charity ball is next
eek. Says you can purchase the raffle tick-

ets online but have to be present to claim th
prize. We have to hurry, though. There are onl
a handful of tickets left."

She turned to stare at him, and he realize
just how close their faces were. Was it his imag
ination, or did she pause ever so slightly whe
their eyes met? Several beats passed as neithe
one of them moved. Finally, she cleared he
throat. "What do you think?"

Think? Drexel was finding it rather hard t
do that at the moment. What exactly was sh
asking him about? Pulling himself together, h
straightened, then winked at her. "Might war
to think about what you'd like to wear. Look
like we're going to a charity ball."

CHAPTER EIGHT

THEY'D BE ATTENDING a ball together. A social event. Like some kind of real couple. Drex was still contemplating the ramifications of that bright and early the next morning when his phone vibrated with a call alert.

He muttered a small curse when the caller's profile picture appeared on his phone screen. Any time the sheikh called for an unscheduled conversation, it usually meant bad news. Another snag in their ongoing negotiations, no doubt.

With a resigned sigh, Drex tapped on the Accept button.

"Sheikh Farhan. To what do I owe the honor?"

There was a long enough pause at the other end that Drex braced himself.

Drex gave him a prod. "Did you have a question about the latest specs?"

He heard the other man sigh through the tiny speaker. "It's not that, Mr. Osoman."

Another bad sign. The sheikh usually called him Drex. "Then…?"

"I've been hearing things."

"What kinds of things?"

"Your personal life is obviously none of m concern."

Yet it seemed it was. Drex racked his brain figure out what the other man might be refe ring to. He hadn't been tied to anyone famo in quite a while. What could the gossip sit possibly be saying about him?

The other man continued. "I believe you' had a major life change recently, correct?"

Marnie. He meant Marnie.

Drex cleared his throat. "Yes. I'm taking ca of my niece for a while. I assure you it will ha no impact on any of my professional duties."

"I would imagine having custody of a sm child would lead to significant distractions. this stage of the deal, we can't afford that, N Osoman."

"We have a nanny. She's highly qualified."

"I see," the sheikh replied. Though, he did really sound like he did. Not at all. "Just o nanny, then?"

"For now."

"Tell me. Does this woman never require a time off? She will never have a personal ma ter to attend to? What if she suddenly quits?"

"She's a live-in," Drex answered, knowir full well how lame that sounded. How it did really answer any of the questions the sheikh had just fired at him.

Drex rubbed his forehead. This was a very competitive deal. Numerous others were waiting in the sidelines to pounce if things went sour between him and the sheikh. On the surface, he had to admit that the other man was right. One live-in nanny hardly appeared as a permanent solution, especially for someone as traditional as the sheikh. More than another employee, what Drexel could really use was a true partner. A wife, almost.

He wanted to laugh out loud. He wasn't even dating anyone at the moment. There was no one who even came close he might consider.

Except maybe there was. Drex stopped short. It was a preposterous idea. Wasn't it? He and Clairey weren't romantically involved. But there was no doubt she already meant more to him and Marnie than a simple employee. There was a world of difference between, say, Sharon, his chef slash house manager, and Clairey.

Romantic or not, he and Clairey were more than boss and employee. And she was certainly more to Marnie than a simple caregiver.

Or maybe he was simply justifying what he was about to do.

"Your Highness, I can assure you the lady in question will not quit."

"How can you be so sure?"

Before he could give himself time to think, Drex found himself uttering a truly remarkable sentence.

"Because we've fallen in love. I intend to ask her to marry me."

The sheikh gasped in response, and Drex went on. "I'm about to present her with a ring any day." What in the world was he doing? Of all the spontaneous, potentially disastrous moves, this one could really bite him in the behind.

But the words were flowing out of him now. Almost unstoppable.

"I was just waiting for the right time and the perfect setting. She's very fond of Marnie and would make an excellent stepmother to her." Technically, all that was true. Not that Drex felt any less deceptive.

"Well, why didn't you say so from the beginning?" the sheikh asked with a pleasant laugh. "Congratulations, my friend. I can't wait to meet your soon-to-be fiancée."

"Meet her?"

"Yes. With the sheikha. I plan on being in New York early next month. For the premiere of a blockbuster I happened to invest in. That superhero franchise. We would love to have you and your lady join us as our guests."

Well, that was certainly an unexpected turn. There was nothing to it. Drex was too far in. He had to accept. He couldn't risk losing his potential business relationship with the sheikh. It was way too important. Especially now. Drex couldn't fail when he'd come this far. "We would consider it an honor."

"Excellent. We shall see you both in a few weeks."

"I look forward to it," Drex said, which this time was indeed a lie. With another muttered curse, he tapped off the call.

What had he just done? And how was he going to present it to Clairey? But was it really that ridiculous a notion? He and Clairey just had to pretend until he could close this deal. Two months at the most. Plus, there was the charity ball next week at the prospective school for Marnie. Wouldn't it look better if they presented themselves as a family unit there? Raffle or not, Marnie had a better chance at being accepted, both literally and figuratively, at a school like that if they didn't have to explain that she was living with a bachelor uncle who barely had time in his life for his own personal needs, let alone the needs of a child.

The ball could be a practice run for their pretend engagement before they met with the sheikh during his visit.

On the surface, what he'd just done made perfect sense. For him, anyway. He just had to hope Clairey would go along with his latest gamble.

* * *

Clearly, she hadn't gotten out of bed this morning. She must still be asleep, and this was all some kind of strange dream. Because there was no way Drex was standing in front of her asking what he appeared to be asking.

"You want to pretend I'm your fiancée?"

"I know it sounds ridiculous."

That was one way to describe it. Clairey focused her gaze to the view of Central Park outside the glass walls. She had to look away. There was no way she could process what was happening if she had to look at Drex. He wanted to take her to some movie premiere. Which was unbelievable enough in itself. But to attend such an event with him as his fiancée—well, that was downright fantastical.

Drex continued. "It's just to appease the sheikh."

She nodded. "Yes. Your client."

"More like *potential business partner*. I really need this deal with him to go through. I know it's a lot to ask."

She held up a hand. He'd been doing his best to explain the reasoning behind such an outrageous ask. But somehow it wasn't quite sinking in.

Her. Clairey Robi. Pretending to be Drexel Osoman's fiancée.

"Tell me again why."

Drex rammed his fingers through his hair. "As you might guess, the sheikh is from a cul-rally very conservative part of the world. When he heard I was the new charge of a little girl, he became concerned it would impact my business dealings. That I'd be distracted."

"So you told him you would soon have a wife."

He nodded. "And, more importantly, a step-mother for a little girl."

"I see."

"Will you do it, Clairey? For the premiere? And maybe also the charity auction for the school? Then we can decide how to go on from there."

She blinked at him. "The auction too?"

He shrugged. "In for a pound and all that. I figured we'd look better as a couple who's trying to get their daughter into a good school. Whether we win or not."

Couple. Parents. Fiancée. The words sounded foreign and strange to her ears. A foolish part of her wished that somehow it could all be real. But that was pure fantasy. Men like Drex didn't fall for women like her. She was small-time. Plain and too ordinary. Of course she wouldn't get any kind of real proposal from a worldly, successful business tycoon.

"If we're lucky, there'll be some media there to leak photos of us together," Drex added.

"You've really thought this through, haven't you?"

He shrugged. "It all seemed to fall into place as I was talking to the sheikh."

What world had she found herself in? Les
than a couple of weeks ago she was sleeping o
a worn-out couch. Now, she was being asked t
play the part of a billionaire's future wife.

Drex went on. "Of course, I will completel
understand if you say no."

Except he didn't look like he would. H
looked completely crestfallen at the possibilit
she might refuse. And what would become o
his crucial business deal if he had to explain t
the sheikh that he didn't in fact have a fiancée
How would he even begin to explain it? Th
amount of embarrassment he would face mad
her shudder. Could she do that to him? After a
he'd done for her?

There was only one clear answer. She shrugge
feigning a nonchalance she didn't feel. "Why not
It's just a couple events. I'll do it."

Drex's mouth widened into a large grin
Without warning, he picked her up and spu
her around in his arms. "For Marnie," he sai
with a chuckle above her head.

Clairey had trouble catching her breath whe
he finally put her back down on her feet. Sh
felt dizzy and light-headed. Couldn't even tel
whether it was due to the spin, the feel of bein
in Drex's arms or the enormity of what she'
just agreed to. Probably all of the above.

For Marnie.

CHAPTER NINE

Clairey resisted the urge to pinch herself as
she stared at her image in the mirror. As cliché
as it was, she felt like Cinderella on her way to
the ball.

It was hard to believe the image in the glass
was actually her. Her dress was unlike anything she'd worn before. A slinky midnight-blue
number that draped over her body with a low-
cut back. Low enough that Clairey had almost
hung it right back up on the rack, but Lana had
insisted it was perfect and jokingly hinted that
Clairey was acting a tad prudish.

For the third time that day, she thanked her
lucky stars for having met Lana when she'd first
arrived. Being a native New Yorker, Lana knew
where to go to find a formal dress at a relative
bargain. The two of them had taken a cab to
the fashion district with their two little charges
in tow. Marnie had been delighted at the adventure.

She'd also borrowed a pair of dark velvet sti-

lettos from the other woman, who luckily ha
the same size feet. The only shoes Clairey ha
brought with her were sensible and practic
ones that someone chasing after an active litt
girl would need. Added to all that, now Lar
was watching Marnie for the night so that sl
and Drexel could attend the charity auction t
gether.

Looking at herself now, Clairey knew she
never be able to adequately thank the oth
woman who was swiftly becoming a true frien

Heavy footsteps sounded outside in the ha
A moment later, there was a soft knock on h
door.

"Come in."

Her door slowly opened, and Drexel stepp
in, preoccupied with adjusting his cuff link
Clairey had to swallow down a gasp. The tu
edo he had on was clearly tailored especially f
him. The suit fit him like glove. His hair w
tidier than usual with a hint of gel. He look
like a prince straight out of a fairy tale.

Her very own Prince Charming. Except I
wasn't really hers. And he never would be.

"Almost ready?" he asked, still tooling arou
with his left cuff link.

"Yes."

He finally looked up at her. His eyes snapp
open wide, then traveled the length of her bod
"Wow!"

Her pulse jumped. Clairey made sure not to react in any way. Though, it was so very hard. It wouldn't do to act pleased at his reaction.

"You look…uh…"

Huh. She'd left him speechless. A twinge of feminine satisfaction hummed along her veins.

"So this will work?" she asked, running a hand along her midsection down toward her thigh.

His response was a very slow nod. "Oh, yeah. That all works. Really, really well."

This time, she couldn't hide her smile.

He blinked a couple more times before giving his head a slight shake. "Oh, before I forget…"

Clairey watched as he reached inside his jacket pocket and pulled out a small square object. A velvet box. Without any kind of preamble, he handed it to her.

"Can't be engaged without a ring."

For a brief moment, she couldn't so much as breathe. Of all the ways she'd imagined receiving an engagement ring, this scenario hadn't entered the realm of her imagination. With trembling fingers, which she hoped Drex didn't notice, she flipped open the cover. Inside on a cloud of white satin fabric sat an oval-cut diamond on a simple gold band. It was beautiful. Suddenly, unexpected tears stung her eyes at how little it really meant. As exquisite as it was, the ring was nothing more than costume jewelry. A prop.

"I guessed on the size," Drex told her. "There's a jeweler next door if it doesn't work. We can do a quick swap." He glanced at his watch. "We'll have just enough time."

Clairey swallowed past the lump in her throat and slid the ring onto her finger. "It's a little snug. But it should work."

"Excellent," Drex said, offering her his arm. "Shall we, then?"

Within minutes, they were down on the street, and Drexel helped her into the waiting limousine.

She studied his profile as the car moved through the city streets. The man was the very definition of drop-dead gorgeous. So handsome in a tux, she was having trouble keeping from gawking at him.

Just for a few moments, she let herself pretend there was more to their relationship than trying to win an auction or a tricky business deal. That she and Drexel were a real couple, that there was no reason for the pretense. The man that would take her back to their shared apartment at the end of the night and kiss her good-night was really hers. Heaven help her, but she did want him to kiss her again. And not just the spontaneous, unplanned kiss he'd planted on her, back on the Cape when she'd accepted his job offer.

A real kiss. She wanted to feel his firm lips on hers. To discover how he might taste. The way his caress would feel.

Stop it.

Clairey could pretend all she wanted. But reality was what it was. This wasn't some kind of real date with her real fiancé. Just like they weren't really engaged. Tonight they were doing all this for Marnie's sake. To try and win her a spot at the school that so many of their building neighbors would be attending. She had absolutely no business fantasizing about the man sitting next to her. He might have paid her a compliment or two, but no doubt Drexel was simply being a gentleman. He was solely focused on the task at hand. As she should be.

Next to her, Drexel cleared his throat. "You look lovely. That dress is very flattering."

So why wasn't he even looking at her as he said so? Regardless, Clairey felt a warm flush creep into her cheeks.

"Thank you. You look quite nice too."

He glanced down at her hands, clasped tight in her lap. She hadn't realized she was holding them so tightly, the new ring biting into the skin of her palm. "Something wrong?"

"No. I'm fine."

He raised an eyebrow. "Are you sure? Because you look like you're on your way to face an inquisition of some sort."

"Okay, I have to admit to being a tad nervous. What if I say the wrong thing to someone or hold my wineglass wrong or something?"

"How in the world might you hold your glass wrong?"

She shrugged. "I don't know. Is my pinkie supposed to be up a certain way?"

"Your pinkie?"

She lifted her hands and waved her two pinkie fingers at him. "The closest I've come to attending an event like this would be the weddings or birthday parties I've worked back at the resort. And for those I was there as an employee."

He reached for her then, gave her hand a reassuring squeeze. "Trust me, no one will be looking at your pinkies. Not in that dress." Clairey inhaled a small gasp at the heat that swam in his eyes as he said the last words. Giving her hands another reassuring squeeze, he dropped them and looked out his window.

It took a lot of willpower to not reach for him again.

The champagne must be going to her head. Because despite being so nervous upon arriving, Clairey was actually starting to have fun. Though, she had to admit, right now that probably had much more to do with the man currently leading her across the dance floor than the bubbly she'd been imbibing. He'd surprised

r soon after they'd arrived by asking her to
nce. Then surprised her further by proving to
e quite competent with his footwork.

Now, they were doing a fast-paced foxtrot
cross the dance floor. Another couple they
ssed actually applauded.

"You know your way around a dance floor,
s. Robi. Is there no end to your talents?"

"With all the weddings I've had to work, you
ck up a few things. You should see my elec-
ic slide."

He winked at her, and a strange feeling of eu-
oria shivered down her spine. "I look forward
it."

"And I could say the same for you. Are you
st a natural, then?"

"Hardly. I dated a competitive ballroom
ncer for a while. At the time, I thought it was
nuisance when she guilted me into learning
e steps. Now I have to admit it's come in quite
ndy over the years."

It was silly, she knew. But the idea of him
ncing with another woman, holding her the
me way he held Clairey right now, had her
spirited.

She had to remind herself that none of this
as real. She was simply pretending. He'd
ted and been involved with more women than
lairey wanted to think about. In real life, a
an like Drexel wouldn't be interested in any

kind of relationship with an ex–resort manage
who he'd simply hired to look after his infor
mally adopted niece.

One waltz and a tango later, they decided
to take their seats. A server stopped by with
tray of the evening's specialty cocktail. Clairey
didn't know what was in it, but it tasted like
sweet ambrosia and honey combined.

From then on, tray after tray arrived with
delicious hors d'oeuvres and tiny dessert tarts
Clairey picked a glazed fruit tart to go with
her cocktail. A burst of flavor exploded on he
tongue at the first bite.

She looked up to find Drexel staring at her
a whimsical smile on his face. "What is it? Do
I have something on my face?"

He chuckled before answering. "No. Just en
joying how much you're enjoying that tart."

A flush warmed her cheeks. "I've always had
a sweet tooth, I'm afraid."

He leaned toward her on the table. "Well
don't keep me waiting. How does it compare
to lobster ice cream?"

Clairey playfully looked upward, as if con-
centrating. "It's a tough call. I might have to
have another tart before I can answer."

Before Drexel could respond, the applauding
couple from the dance floor approached their
table and asked to join them. Drexel nodded
without hesitation and motioned for them to

pull out a chair. Silly as it was, Clairey had to squash a surge of disappointment. It was rather fun having Drexel to herself, and the intrusion felt like a rare and precious gift had been taken away from her.

She forced a smile on her face as the introductions were made.

"You don't look familiar," the woman said now. "Is your child new to the school?"

"No. We're hoping she will be," Drexel answered.

"Ah, you're here for the raffle, then."

"We are."

"Well, best of luck to you," the husband said. "I hope your daughter gets in."

Drexel didn't bother to correct the other man. Instead, he pulled her ever so slightly closer, his arm tightening around her shoulders. A shiver of heat ran down her spine at the contact. Along with a thread of excitement. There was something oddly enticing about the fact that this other couple, as well as the other people in the room, must assume they were married with a child of their own. She had no business feeling so fond of that idea, but she couldn't deny that she was.

Her phone pinged with a text message right at that moment. "Excuse me, but I must check this," she said to the table at large and pulled out her phone.

"It's Lana," she said to Drexel a moment late

Tight lines of concern immediately etched h
face. "Is everything all right, darling?"

Clairey's heart quickened at the endearmen
She nodded, brushing aside the longing that ha
bloomed in her chest at the name he'd calle
her. All this pretending was starting to feel a
too real for her emotions. "Yes, yes. Everythir
is fine. She says the girls are asking if Marn
might spend the night. They'd like a sleepover

His outward breath of relief was audibl
"Fine by me."

Clairey sent a quick text response to Lana.

"Your sitter for the evening?" the wife aske

I'm actually the sitter was the first thoug]
that popped into her head, reminding her of r
ality once more. "She's more a close friend
Clairey answered, which was the absolute trut

The woman gave her a soft smile in respons
just as the lights dimmed. A bolt of exciteme
lanced through Clairey's chest. It was time f
the raffle. A large screen drew down on th
wall behind the stage. Digital icons scrambl
around and around until eventually one lit u
as the winner.

Clairey gasped with delight as she read tw
words on the screen. *Marnie Osoman.*

Before she knew it, Drexel stood at her sid
pulling her chair out. His excitement was pa
pable. "We won. Marnie won!"

"I know! I can hardly believe it." Had that really just happened?

"We did this together." Clairey gasped as he picked her up off her feet and twirled her around just as he had three days ago when he'd first proposed his outrageous fake-engagement plan. Her pulse, already pounding by the time he put her back down, skyrocketed at his next words. "We make a good team, my love."

Everything Drexel had ever acquired throughout his life had come from hard work and sheer drive. Having something he'd wanted so badly randomly come to be through mere chance was a heady feeling he hadn't been adequately prepared for.

Now, as he escorted Clairey into the back of their waiting limo, a disquieting thought occurred to him. One some deep level, he might begin to understand the temptations that could have led his father into a life of excessive and destructive gambling.

The thrill he'd just felt in there when Marnie's name was announced, the chances he took in boardrooms—hell, look at the huge gamble he'd taken by fibbing to the sheikh. Was he more like his old man than he might have thought? Drexel pushed the disturbing thoughts aside and strode to the other side of the car to slide into the back seat next to Clairey. He refused to entertain any unpleasant thought at the moment. What had just happened in there with the draw was cause for celebration.

He turned to tell Clairey exactly that. Her smile hadn't faded in the least. She was humming with excitement and happiness. He might even say she was happier for Marnie than even he was.

"I say this calls for champagne. What do you say?"

"She'll be so happy when we tell her the news."

Drexel had to laugh. Her focus was squarely on Marnie. As well it should be at a time like this. But had she even heard what he'd asked about celebrating?

"Well?" he prodded.

She nodded with enthusiasm. "Yes. Let's toast to Marnie's good luck this evening. I'm guessing you have a good bottle of champagne back at the apartment."

She'd be guessing right. But Drexel had something else in mind. He'd been thinking since that first night about how much she'd enjoyed watching the Manhattan skyline out of his penthouse glass wall.

"I was thinking we'd stay out a little longer," he answered her.

Her eyebrows lifted slightly. "You were?"

"Seeing as Marnie's settled for the night.

There's a place I wanted to take you. I think you'll enjoy it."

Within minutes, they'd arrived at the spot. Drexel escorted Clairey out of the car and to the lobby of the five-star restaurant they'd pulled up to.

They were greeted immediately upon walking through the revolving glass doors.

A familiar smiling face approached and led them to the hostess stand. "Will you be dining with us tonight, Mr. Osoman? Your table can be set up in moments."

"Just here for a nightcap, Kristen."

The young woman returned the thick leather menus back to their slot. "Enjoy your night."

"The restaurant has rooftop seating," he explained to Clairey. "As well as a fully stocked bar. And given that it's a Saturday evening, there should be live entertainment."

Drexel led Clairey toward the elevator with a hand to her back. He had to suck in a breath at the touch of his skin against her bare back. The low-cut dress she wore screamed temptation, and he couldn't seem to resist touching her. Having her up against him on the dance floor had given him a taste of the way she felt in his arms. Heaven help him, it had felt right. He wanted to dance with her again, to touch her again.

He wanted it very much.

This was a mistake. Drexel knew he was bound to regret it as soon as the night was over. But was it so wrong just to live in the moment for once in his life? A look at the excitement on Clairey's face as the elevator lifted higher and higher gave him a clear answer to that question.

It was confirmed when they reached the part of the ride up where the steel walls gave way to glass. She gasped as the view of the city below and Central Park in the distance burst into view. She actually pressed her palms against the glass and studied the scene below as they continued to rise up. "Oh, my."

He'd seen the view from this elevator countless times in the past. Something about the way Clairey was reacting to it now made him wonder just how much he'd actually seen it. The way the greenery of the park stuck out like a portrait landscape within the gray tone of the city. How the horse-drawn carriages looked like miniature toys from this height. How the lights from the neighboring buildings lit up the sky. He'd never really looked at any of that before.

That was the thing about Clairey: she made him appreciate things he might not otherwise even notice. Like she had with helping his niece adjust to her new life. It would have never occurred to him that she might need a friend her own age until school started. Nor would it have occurred to him to research some of the items e'd seen on her computer that day about Marie's developmental or nutritional needs.

"This is breathtaking," she said now, her gaze till fixed on the glass panel. "I can see why you ome here often."

"What makes you think I come here often?"

"The hostess down there said you had a regular table."

He didn't bother to correct her. He happened o have a table because he owned the restaurant. n fact, he owned the commercial building itelf, which housed everything from boutiques nd jewelry shops on the first floor to some of ie most upscale apartments in New York City.

But none of that was the reason he felt like a ortunate man tonight. That feeling was due to ie woman he'd be lucky enough to spend the vening with.

CHAPTER TEN

SHE'D STEPPED INTO another world. How coul
this possibly be the top of a building? Clairey
felt as if she'd somehow taken an elevator to a
island in the Caribbean. Trees two to three time:
her height outlined the square area. Across from
where they stood, the bar Drexel mentioned wa
a U-shaped high-top structure about thirty fee
in length. It was surrounded by throngs of peo
ple. A four-piece band right next to it played a
bouncy, jazzy number that had her tapping he
feet. A lit pool complete with a waterfall com
pleted the picture.

The only thing missing was a sandy beach
and the ocean.

She lost count of the number of times she'
felt awestruck this evening. A server approache
them almost immediately.

"The usual, Mr. Osoman? And what can I ge
for the lady?"

He really must come here a lot. But who coul
blame him? The place was beyond entertain

ng. She'd come here every night if she could. Though, something told her she wouldn't be able to afford it. Not if she wanted to continue paying down those student loans.

Drexel ordered a bottle of something that sounded French before leading her to a high-top table by the pool.

"This is bigger than the pool deck area back at the Sea View," she said as he pulled out a stool for her and helped her sit.

He took the other stool across from her but removed his tuxedo jacket first. Then he proceeded to roll the sleeves of his shirt up to below his elbows. Something about his bare arms sent a shiver of electricity over her skin. He'd already unbuttoned the top of his collar midway to his chest. The man looked downright dashing whenever he loosened his collar and rolled his sleeves up that way.

Clairey made herself look away and focus on the small crowd of dancers in front of the band. The server from earlier arrived and ceremoniously uncorked a sweating, green-tinged bottle with a foreign label. The only word she could make out was *champagne*.

Drexel lifted his glass to hers after the young woman was done serving and had walked away with a slight bow. "To Marnie and the new life she's about to embark on in New York."

Clairey tapped her flute to his and added "And to the luck of the draw."

"I'll drink to that."

She took a small sip. Tiny bubbles burst o her tongue and a wave of exquisite flavor rushe her taste buds. She held the glass out and ex amined it. "Wow."

"You like it?"

That was an understatement. It was dowr right shocking just how much she liked it. "I'v had sparkling wine before. The real thing quite a whole other level, isn't it?"

"Nothing compares to the real thing. Goo or bad."

It sounded like a very loaded statemen Though, for the life of her, she couldn't gues what he might be referring to.

He continued before she could so much think of how to go about asking.

"So, tell me about yourself, Ms. Robi. It o curs to me that I don't know all that much abo you."

That was rich. At least he knew where sh was from and how she'd come about to lose h coveted job. She didn't know a thing about hin Only that he'd grown up in New Jersey some where near Atlantic City.

She tapped a finger to her chin with moc seriousness. "Let's see. Upon the time of ou meeting back in Cape Cod, Massachusetts, I foolishly risked my job which led to all sorts of financial instability. But you know all about that."

"Ah, but there's a lot I don't know."

She eyed him over her glass. "For instance?"

"For instance, is there anyone back on Cape Cod who might feel slighted if they happen to catch a photo of you on the arm of someone claiming to be your fiancé?"

Clairey had to chuckle at the question. "Is that your roundabout way of asking me if I'm involved with anyone?"

He ducked his head with a sheepishness that only seemed to add to his charm. "Guilty as charged."

She swallowed another sip of her drink. "There's nothing to tell. I haven't been serious with anyone. Not really. Just a few dates here and there." She squeezed her eyes shut before divulging the rest. "And there was a certain Casanova in college who said all the right things, then ghosted me."

Clairey cringed internally at the memory of her college crush. For the first time since losing her father, she'd thought when she'd met him that maybe she'd found someone who might be able to love her. She'd been so naive.

"Then, he was beyond a fool," Drex said, his voice thick. He raised his glass. "And look where you are now."

In some kind of fantasy, apparently. One where she got to pretend she might actually become this man's wife in some unknown universe.

There was a thing or two she was curious about too. She braced herself to ask the question that had been forming on the tip of her tongue since they'd first sat down. "What did you mean before, when you said what you did about things that are real being good or bad?"

He shrugged. "Take Marnie, for instance. I'm not her real father. One might argue she's unfortunate in that she's stuck with an uncle when her actual dad is fully capable of parenting her. So she's stuck with second best."

"You can't honestly feel like you're second-best where Marnie is concerned."

He swirled the liquid in his glass, took another sip. "Chase wasn't perfect as a father. But he is her real dad. That's just a matter of fact."

Her heart tugged a little in her chest. She'd had no idea he was harboring any sense of inadequacy as far as Marnie was concerned.

"Oh, Drexel, you can't think that way. Look how much you're doing for her. And she's thriving in New York."

"But she misses her dad. Tells me so every night when I tuck her into bed."

She'd been telling Clairey as well. "That's only natural and to be expected. Her longing for her dad in no way diminishes all that you've done to make her feel settled here."

His response was a tight frown. He was second-guessing himself. And he really had no cause to. Clairey would have never pegged Drexel Osoman as the insecure type. But apparently, at least in this one area, he was.

"I hope you're right, Clairey. I really do."

Without thinking, she reached for him then. Leaning over the table, she took one of his hands in both of hers. His gaze followed to where they touched, and heat swam in his eyes.

Yet she couldn't bring herself to pull away.

Her hands felt good on his. And it felt good to sit here with her now, simply chatting. Drexel hadn't intended to reveal any of his feelings about being unexpectedly responsible for his niece. But it felt good to get it off his chest. Something about Clairey felt familiar, put him at ease talking about things he'd normally keep close to his chest. He'd grown to feel affection for her. It was more than merely sharing a living space. Which reminded him...

"I've been meaning to tell you, and I hope it goes without saying, you're welcome to have visitors at the penthouse. There must be friends or relatives you'll be missing. Invite whoever you'd like. Whenever. This is your home now too."

Clairey smiled at him. "That's very kind of

you. Thank you. There is someone I might have come see me."

"Oh?"

She nodded. "A friend. Tessa would get such a kick out of staying in New York for a few days." Her eyes widened slightly. "Though, I'm not quite sure what I would tell her about this." She held her hand up to indicate the fake-engagement ring.

"I'll leave that up to you. She's your friend. You decide what you want her to know."

Her shoulders sagged with relief. "I'm glad you feel that way. I wouldn't feel right lying to Tessa. And I know I can trust her."

"Then, I trust you to make that call."

"Thank you for that," she said, her smile warm. "Wait until she gets a load of the penthouse. She won't believe what luxury I'm living in."

He had to chuckle at that. Sometimes Drexel forgot just how much he had to be grateful for and how much he took for granted in his life.

"So just Tessa, then?"

She teased her bottom lip with her tongue. "I think so. For now."

"What about your mom? You said you haven't seen her in a few years. You might have a reunion of sorts."

Drexel felt like a heel as soon as the words left his mouth. Though he was sincere about

elcoming any guest of Clairey's, the truth was
: was curious about her. He wanted to know
ore. Like exactly why she hadn't seen her
other in so long.

"My mom will be too busy to visit," she an-
vered after a long pause, her voice laced with
tin.

Yep, he definitely was a heel to pick at her
ab that way.

Clairey continued. "She and Frank do a lot
RVing and camping. They don't have much
om in their lives for anyone else."

Or room in their hearts, it sounded like. "The
ɔmad life."

"Something like that."

"Sounds like you miss her."

She ducked her head slightly. "I did at first.
ve grown to accept it over the years. My mom
as never the nurturing type to begin with. She
ɛrtainly didn't really have much use for me
ter my father passed."

"How long have you been on your own?"

She swallowed. "I felt alone from the mo-
ent my dad died. But things really came to a
:ad in our household once I turned eighteen."

"How so?"

"Frank always acted like he resented me. I
n't recall a single instance where he was kind.
 fact, he seemed to go out of his way to be
uel."

Drexel itched to take her into his arms and soothe some of her pain away. He had no doubt that she would accept his comfort. But right now, at this moment, it was more important that she say as much as she wanted to tell him about her past. "In what ways?" he asked.

"He'd comment about my hair, my clothing. Make disparaging remarks about my looks. Say things like I definitely didn't take after my mother as she was pretty and I was...well, the opposite of that."

Anger surged in his chest. Something told him her stepfather had less than innocuous reasons for noticing and commenting on her looks. Drexel never felt such animosity toward a man he had never met. This Frank had better hope the two of them never happened to cross paths. "He'd always object if I wanted to bring friends home. And if any came to the house, he'd make sure to make them feel unwelcome and uncomfortable. I started to lose touch with the few friends I had, thanks to him."

"What happened when you turned eighteen?"

Clairey closed her eyes and blew out a slow breath. "He woke up in a particularly sour mood. Grumbling about how I was always in his way, I wasn't doing enough around the house. You get the picture."

He certainly did. And it had him nearly shaking with rage.

Clairey went on. "I had the audacity to talk back. I said something like how the house was a mess because he never picked up after himself, leaving dirty dishes and filthy ashtrays all over the place." Her hand tightened around the stem of her flute. "My mom came in then. I knew she wouldn't defend me, she never had. But I still had some small smidgen of hope." She huffed out an ironic chuckle.

"What did she do?"

"My stepfather just said it. He told her he wanted me gone. That I was of age now, I had no business in his house. Never mind that it wasn't his house at all. He'd moved into the house my parents had bought together when they were first married."

Drexel had to lean back in his chair. He couldn't help but imagine his own niece in such a situation. How close had the girl come to experiencing such an existence? What would have happened if he hadn't been around when Chase's new wife made her wishes clear about not wanting a child underfoot? But this was about Clairey. He waited silently for her to tell him the rest.

She took another small sip of wine before doing so. "I remember thinking, *This is it*. We'd finally be rid of him. My mother wouldn't let him give such an ultimatum."

His heart sank for her as he could only guess

what must have played out afterward. "I take
that's not what happened."

"You'd be guessing right. My mother's reac‐
tion was not what I'd expected. Though, I se
now how naive I was to be shocked."

It took several moments, but she went o‐
"She turned to me and said five simple word
'You need to go, Clairey.'"

She immediately turned away, but not befor
he noticed the wetness flooding her eyes. "Th‐
was the last night I spent in my childhood home

Drexel bit back a curse. She deserved s
much more than the hand she'd been dealt. N
wonder she felt such a connection to Marn
and was so quickly forming a bond with he
Clairey could relate to the little girl. She'd e‐
sentially been abandoned herself.

Clairey toyed with the bangs on her forehea‐
"Well, that was quite a trip down memory lane
she said with an unconvincing smile. "I didn
mean to dump so much sad history on you. O
such a pleasant night too."

"I'm glad you told me, Clairey." People didn
tend to confide in him. He was glad Claire
seemed to be an exception.

Several wisps of hair had come loose an
blew softly in the wind. It took every ounc
of willpower he possessed not to reach ove
and tuck those strands back into place. The
he'd run his finger down her cheek, trail h

hand lower toward her chest. The round table between them was small enough that she was easily within reach.

The band behind them started a new number, and Clairey turned her head in their direction. "I really like this song. Are you up for any more dancing tonight?"

He knew an attempt to change the subject when he heard one. After all, he was a master at it himself.

He stood and extended his hand out to her. "I'd be honored."

Clairey tried not to react to the electricity that hummed through her as Drexel took her by the elbow to lead her to the square dance floor. She couldn't believe how much of herself and her past she'd just shared with him. Not even Tessa had heard as much about her life before she'd moved out of her childhood home. It wasn't something she particularly enjoyed talking about. But something about Drexel had made her feel open and comfortable enough to share it all with him.

Ironic, really. Of all the ways she could describe how she felt about the man, *comfortable* would probably not even make the list.

Excited. Aware. Attracted. Those words definitely would.

Now, as they moved together to the bouncy

song, she noticed how in sync they were, how well they moved together. She felt lighter, somehow. As if a weight had been lifted off her chest. Talking to Drexel about Frank and her mother had been freeing. Cathartic. She'd had no idea how much she'd wanted to share it all with someone. Although she'd never felt the need to do so before. Something had told her that Drexel would understand, in a way that she was certain even Tessa wouldn't be able to.

No. Drexel was unlike anyone she could think of.

Without even meaning to, she found herself voicing her thoughts aloud. "You're not like any man I've ever met." She cringed as soon as the words left her mouth. Of all the cliché-sounding… Made all the worse as she'd yelled the words over the loud music. She could have sworn she heard someone on the dance floor behind her snicker.

Clairey wanted to somehow take the words back and simultaneously disappear into a sinkhole. She ducked her head as heat rushed to her cheeks.

Drexel apparently noticed. "Don't be embarrassed, Clairey. I was thinking the very same thing about you."

She blinked. "Me?"

As luck would have it, the current song ended right at that moment. The next tune was much slower. Drexel didn't seem to hesitate. She found herself in his arms, nestled against his chest as he moved with her to the music. The scent of him, now so familiar, washed over her. A combination of some kind of aftershave that reminded her of moonlit summer nights along with the distinctive masculine scent that was his alone.

"Yes, you," he said against her, ducking slightly to accommodate their height difference.

He had to be patronizing her, trying to make her feel better, given what she'd told him. The man had dated supermodels, actresses and world-renowned dancers. Clairey was certainly different than any of those types, but not in any kind of impressive way. "You don't have to do that, Drexel. You don't have to try and indulge me with platitudes."

He sighed, his breath hot against her cheek. A shudder ran through her at the feel of him so close.

"You beautiful, silly little fool. You don't believe me, do you?"

"I can't say that I do," she admitted.

She felt his arms around her tighten ever so slightly. Her heart pounded double-time in her chest at the closer contact.

"Then, let me try to explain," he said. "For one, you made it by yourself after losing everything you'd known to become the manager of a world-class resort."

She scoffed. "I lost that job, remember?"

"I do. I recall you lost the job because you stuck your neck out for a little girl you didn't even know. You're doing everything you can now to make sure that little girl thrives and flourishes."

"Many others would have done so. Doesn't make me special in any way."

"You can't believe that." He tilted her chin with his finger, staring into her eyes. "Listen. I have no idea what I would have done without you. Finding the school for Marnie. Enabling her to make a friend. Helping me keep this business deal going by pretending to be in love with me."

Her voice caught at his last few words. He might be pretending. But the imaginary line for her was becoming more and more blurry by the instant.

"So yes, in my eyes that makes you one exceptional, impressive young woman."

He sounded so genuine. The words he said were beyond touching. So why did she feel like crying? She couldn't come up with anything to say in response.

Because she wanted more, heaven help her.

"Thank you, Drexel," she said softly when she finally found her voice.

"For what? Telling you the truth about your-self?"

The truth as he saw it, anyway. She still wasn't convinced she was as impressive as he'd just made her sound. "Yes," she admitted. "I had no idea how badly I needed to hear it."

"You're welcome," he answered simply. They danced together in silence for two more songs. Clairey allowed herself to fully indulge in the sensations she was experiencing: the feel of him against her body, his heartbeat pulsing against her upper chest, the strength she felt emanating from him and somehow bolstering her own.

By the time she looked up, the night had grown much later, and the crowd had considerably thinned. The band played their last song and said their good-nights.

A sense of sadness washed over her: she didn't want this night to end. "Looks like most people are heading out along with the band. Maybe we should call it a night."

Drexel glanced at his watch. "Nonsense. The night is just beginning."

When they returned to their table, another chilled bottle had been opened, and the ice bucket filled with fresh ice. Additionally, a bowl of fresh berries had been placed in the center with a small pitcher of chocolate sauce.

He must be quite a favored customer, the way the staff seemed to be catering to him. Drexel

took one of the larger berries and dipped it i
the sauce. He held it out to Clairey. She opene
her lips and accepted the treat. The flavor o
the fresh fruit mixed with deep rich chocolat
had her taste buds celebrating. "Hmmm. That'
delicious."

Drexel picked up the bowl of fruit and sauc
and walked over to an area by the pool with
set of chaise longues.

Clairey indulged in a few more of the berries
admiring the view of the starlit sky. For severa
moments, they simply relaxed there, lying sid
by side.

When she thought to look, there was no on
left but staff. And they seemed to be clearin
up the place. "Shouldn't we be going too? The
seem to be closing up shop."

He nodded his head. "They won't mind i
we linger."

They certainly didn't seem to mind at all. I
fact, no one was even paying attention to them

Maybe it was the champagne. Or maybe i
was the way he'd made her feel back on th
dance floor. But a courageous part of he
seemed to rise to the surface.

She wanted Drexel to kiss her. For once in he
life, she was going to ask for what she wanted

She summoned all the courage she could
"You apologized to me that day. About kiss
ing me."

He turned to fully face her. "Yes. I shouldn't have done that."

"I liked it, Drex," she admitted, her heart ready to pound out of her chest. Heat darkened his eyes. "I'd like you to kiss me again. Now."

He didn't hesitate. With a gentle grip on her forearm, he pulled her toward him. Then his lips were on hers.

This kiss was entirely different than the quick, chaste one he'd planted on her back on the Cape. No, this one was far from chaste. It was fire and desire and pure passion.

It would take a while to calm her racing pulse.

CHAPTER ELEVEN

CLAIREY AWOKE WITH a start as the first rays of predawn sun landed softly on her face. Heaven help her, somehow she'd fallen asleep. Not only that, she'd done so in Drexel's arms, lying next to him in the very same lounge chair. They were the only two people left on the roof. His tuxedo jacket covered her middle, his arms wrapped around her shoulders. She bolted upright.

What in the world had come over her to fall asleep like that? That did it: she was never drinking champagne again. Then the other memory rushed through her mind. The kiss. She'd nestled up against Drexel after that mind-blowing kiss. No wonder she'd lost all her senses.

He stirred next to her now. She waited with bated breath as he finally opened his eyes.

His eyes widened when they landed on her face. "What's the matter? You look like you've been caught with your hand in the cookie jar."

"What do you mean, what's the matter? We fell asleep up here."

An alarming thought shot through her and turned her blood ice-cold. What if something had gone wrong during the night and Lana had tried to reach her? They might have been fast asleep when Marnie needed them. She rummaged around for her handbag until she located it hanging from the armrest of the lounger. Luckily, her phone displayed no missed messages when she pulled it out and looked at the screen.

Relief rushed through her, and she let out a long sigh. "I can't believe we might have missed a call from Lana."

He lifted an eyebrow. "Did you intend to stay up the whole night back at the penthouse in case she called?"

"Well, no, but…"

"How is falling asleep here any different?"

Well, when he put it that way… "I don't know."

He leaned back against the chair and pulled her back along with him. "Try to relax. Look," he said and pointed to the horizon.

Clairey glanced at the sky, then had to rub her eyes to get a better look. The sight took her breath away. The sun rising in the distant sky sat among a burst of orange and red. The view looked like it could have been hand-painted by a gifted artist. At this height, it was as if they were aligned perfectly with the magnificent sight.

"Wow," was all she could muster.

Drexel's hand tightened around her shoulder. "The view of the sunrise from a New York City high-rise is a wonder to behold. And you would have missed it if we hadn't fallen asleep up here."

She couldn't tear her gaze away from the sky. "Still, it feels wrong to have stayed up here all this time. Won't anyone say anything?"

He shrugged. "They'd have no standing to. I own the place."

Had she just heard him right? "You own the restaurant and the bar?"

"Sort of."

What did that mean? He either owned the establishment or he didn't. "I don't understand."

He tapped her nose playfully before standing up and stretching. "I own the building. As well as everything in it."

Clairey watched in awe as Drexel pulled a key card out of his wallet and used it to summon the rooftop elevator. A whirring, mechanical sound echoed from the floors below. Moments later, the double doors slid open, and Drexel gestured for her to step inside.

He owned the building. And the businesses and apartments within. That certainly explained the deference he'd been shown by the staff all night. As well as how comfortable he was to stay here overnight.

Why was she even surprised?

He used the same key card to engage the panel of buttons on the wall of the elevator. Within seconds they were on the ground floor and exiting to the street.

They summoned a taxi to bring them back to his building. The events of the past several hours ran through her mind like scenes from a movie as they entered the lobby. If the doorman and desk attendant noticed they were still clad in evening attire, they had the grace to look away with just a brief, friendly smile.

Had she really just lived through such a romantic and magical night? Had she really had the nerve to ask Drex to kiss her? And he'd obliged. She rubbed her fingers along her lips summoning the feel of his mouth against hers.

Clairey knew it had all indeed happened. But she also knew she couldn't let any of it go to her head. Not even the kiss. Especially not the kiss.

It didn't mean anything. Not to him. The fantasy and magic of the evening, along with all the pretending, had gone to both their heads. As soon as Marnie returned to the apartment, Clairey would go right back to being the hired help. The kiss last night and everything that had happened both before and after were merely her living out fantasies she had no business entertaining in the first place.

She had a more pressing matter to deal with when the elevator doors opened to reveal a familiar face. Lana did a double take when she saw them.

"Oh, hey."

"Um…hello."

"My *Sunday Times* wasn't outside the door," she said. "I just popped down to see if any papers had arrived at the building. The girls are still sound asleep," she added after several silent beats.

"Oh," was all Clairey could come up with to say. No doubt, she'd face a barrage of questions from the other woman as soon as the two of them found themselves alone. For the life of her, she had no idea what she might say in response. How could she address Lana's questions when she didn't know the answers herself?

Drexel seemed to be shifting his glance from one woman to the other, a curious expression on his face. He was the one who finally broke the awkward silence.

"I take it the girls had a fun night together?" he addressed Lana with a charming smile.

Lana blinked as if confused. Then she seemed to pull herself together. "Oh! Yes! Yes, they had a lot of fun. They can't wait to do it again sometime." She waved a hand in their general direc-

on. "We'd love to have her. You know, if you
vo want to go out again."

Drexel's smile widened. Clairey cringed
here she stood. She knew her friend meant
ell, but her words made for the most awkward
moments. "I'm sure that won't be ne—"

Drexel cut her off before she could finish.
We just might take you up on that. Thank you."
Now she was practically gawking.

Lana blinked some more before giving her
ead a brisk shake. "Well, I guess I'll go see
out my paper, then." She brushed by them
t then suddenly turned again. "Oh, I chatted
ith my sister yesterday. She says a new litter
calicos just arrived the other day. They're
oking for fosters or adopters."

It took Clairey a moment to shift her focus
the sudden turn in the conversation. Kittens.
e and Drexel had promised Marnie they'd get
r a pet.

"Oh, that's good news."

Lana nodded. "You and Marnie can even head
own there later today to take a look. They're
en for a few hours after lunch on Sundays.
s said she'd personally introduce them to you."

"That's very nice of her," Clairey answered.

Drexel rubbed a hand over the dark stubble
his chin. "Wait a minute. I have a small ob-
ction."

Clairey's stomach fell. He'd changed his mind

about the pet. Marnie was going to be heartbroken. "You do?"

He nodded at her solemnly. "Why should you ladies have all the fun? I'd like to meet these little creatures too."

It was Clairey's turn to blink in confusion. "You want to come with us? To look at kittens?"

He narrowed his eyes. "Why's that so hard to believe?"

Lana guffawed, then coughed into her hand to try and cover it. She was thinking exactly what Clairey was. In no sense whatsoever did Drexel Osoman give off the impression that he might waste away the afternoon playing with a litter of kittens.

"You're just always so busy on Sundays," Clairey answered. "Getting ready for the work week ahead."

"Yes, well. Some things a man should make time for."

He was going to make time to help them pick out a kitten.

How in the world had he found himself here?

Drexel knew the answer, and he had to acknowledge it. Sure, he wanted to be here for his niece. But the real reason for his motivation currently stood off in the corner of the room. She'd changed into a sundress that draped her curves.

in all the right ways. Her sandals showed off rainbow-painted toenails.

Not nearly as splashy an outfit as what she'd worn last night, yet somehow just as tantalizing. The woman could wear a straw bag and it would look tantalizing on her.

But there was more to her that drew him.

He had to admit he wanted to continue spending time with Clairey. He'd enjoyed himself last night more than he had in a long time. As long as he could remember. In fact, he couldn't recall ever previously feeling so carefree, so content just to live in the moment and enjoy the company of the woman he was with.

She brought out a playful side of him he'd thought he'd lost years ago. Drex couldn't even explain why. He just knew he felt lighter around her, less like the whole world rested on his shoulders.

Drexel picked up the small mound of fluff trying desperately to climb up on his shoe only to fail miserably. If someone had told him a month ago that he'd be at a city animal shelter as small kittens tried to climb on him, he would have laughed at the image. The tiny thing wiggled in his palm, waiving his little stub of a tail. Drexel didn't think anything could feel quite so soft.

"Do you like that one, Uncle Drexel?" Marnie asked, her own arms holding a bundle of squirming mewing furry babies.

"I do. And he seems to like me."

Clairey stood off in the corner, her arm crossed and an amused smile on her face. She was taking it all in and seemed wholly entertained. "They all seem to like you," she said. Then her smile faded. "Except this one." She walked over to one of the kittens shivering by itself in the corner. The poor thing looked scared to death. It was barely half the size of the rest of the litter. Clairey gave its tiny head a gentle rub with her thumb.

"That one is dealing with a bit of a health issue," the lab tech, who was also Lana's sister, informed them.

Clairey looked up at her with alarm. "What kind of health issue?"

"She was born with a congenital defect. An umbilical hernia. She struggles to eat. It's why she's so much smaller."

"Is there a way to cure her?" Clairey asked the other woman.

"We're hoping she'll grow out of it. She's on some meds in the meantime. Otherwise, she may need surgery at some point."

Marnie gently put down the three kittens she'd been holding and immediately walked over to the ill one with Clairey.

"Oh, the poor thing," his niece cried, a hitch

in her voice. "She looks so frightened." She ran a hand softly along the cat's back.

Clairey looked ready to cry herself. She helped Marnie pick up the kitten and gently hold her against her chest. The cat immediately started to purr.

One look at the two human and one feline females, and Drexel knew what he had to do. "That's the one we'll take, then."

As soon as the words left his mouth, another little one scurried over to Clairey's sandaled feet. Though still low and soft, its mewing had definitely grown in intensity.

Marnie glanced down at the new arrival, and her eyes welled up with tears. "They don't want to be separated."

The lab tech tilted her head. "You're a very insightful little girl, Marnie." She nodded toward the two kittens. "Those two are nearly inseparable. They cuddle together for naps and cry whenever the other is being handled."

Drexel studied the scene before him. Clairey rubbing a hand down Marnie's back to comfort her in her distress over the plight of the cat siblings. The shivering little one mewing desperately for his sister. Then he glanced down at the wiggling ball of fur he still held in his own hand.

Again, the decision was clear. There was nothing for it. They would have to get all three.

* * *

The moment of truth was here. Or the moment of falsehood. Clairey couldn't even be sure which. All she knew was that in a few short minutes she'd be meeting a real-life sheikh and his wife. And she'd have to do so while pretending she was about to become a wife herself.

If she was nervous before the school auction, what she felt now was close to sheer panic.

She should be excited, she really should. After all, she was currently sitting in the back of a stretch limo next to Drex en route to Times Square. For an exclusive screening of the latest installment of a major superhero franchise she'd barely paid attention to in her past life as a resort manager. Most women would be giddy. But all she could think about was saying or doing the wrong thing and blowing the whole charade completely.

Drex must have sensed her trepidation. "Try to relax, Clairey. Everything will be fine. The sheikh and his wife are actually lovely people. If a little sober."

"I'll try," was the only response she could utter.

Drex reached over and gave her hand a reassuring squeeze. "Just trust me."

She did. She just wasn't sure if she could trust herself. Within minutes they'd reached the long line of luxury cars being directed toward the entrance of the theater. Finally, the limo came to a complete stop, and an attendant immediately appeared near her door and began to open it.

Drex turned to her. "Ready?"

"As I'll ever be."

He'd reached her side of the car before she'd so much as stepped foot outside the vehicle.

A roar of noise greeted her ears once they were outside. Throngs of people had gathered across the street which had been cordoned off. Clairey's steps faltered as she took in the size of the crowd.

"It's okay, sweetheart," Drex said in her ear calmly. "They're here to see the real talent. The stars haven't arrived yet. No one is paying attention to us."

The attendant motioned for them to follow and quickly led them past the crowds and inside the building. By the time they reached the lobby, Clairey thought her heart might very well beat right out of her chest.

Before she could so much as try to take a steadying breath, they were immediately approached by an elegant-looking older couple dressed in traditional ceremonial dress. The sheikh and his wife. They were surrounded by a quartet of burly-looking men in tuxedos and earpieces. She'd never met anyone who'd needed bodyguards before.

She mimicked Drex's slight bow of his head in greeting just as he'd instructed her to do.

"Lovely to see you, Drex," the sheikh said before turning to her. "And so lovely to meet you."

Clairey could barely keep from trembling with apprehension as the formal introductions were made. But by the time they'd taken their seats and the theater lights dimmed around them, the sheikha had completely charmed her. The woman was warm and genial and more relatable than Clairey would have ever guessed.

It took a while, but eventually Clairey even managed to relax enough to enjoy the movie. Surprising, as her tastes usually ran more along rom-coms and less action-packed entertainment.

But then she lost all sense of focus again when she felt Drex's arm come around her shoulder. He gave her a gentle squeeze and surprised her further by dropping a series of gentle kisses along her cheek, then lower along her jaw.

She couldn't help her gasp as heat curled low in her belly and spread through her limbs. The man's touch did things to her that she couldn't begin to understand. If they were alone at that moment, she'd have half a mind to jump on his lap and kiss him until they both lost all sense.

She felt his breath against her cheek as he leaned close to whisper something in her ear. When he spoke, it took her a minute to process

xactly what he was telling her. "I just got a
ext on my phone during that last quiet scene.
heikh Farhan wants to move forward. Says
e's ready to sign off on it all. I have you to
ank, Clairey."

Clairey's skin grew cold. So that's what the
how of affection had really been about. Drex
vas merely doing it all for the sheikh's benefit.
o show him that they were indeed a besotted
ouple in love and that he could be comfortable
ith the decision to do business with Drex. His
enderness, the loving caress and gentle kisses
ad nothing at all to do with her.

The night of the auction, she'd been the one
vho'd asked him to kiss her. This time, it was
ruse for the benefit of his potential business
artner. What did that say about the way he felt
bout her?

A brick of disappointment settled in her stom-
ch, and her eyes began to sting at the crushing
ealization. She would have kicked herself for
if she could.

It looked like Drex's plan had worked like a
harm. Too bad she'd forgotten for a moment
at plan was the only reason she was here with
im in the first place.

CHAPTER TWELVE

Three months later

DREXEL CALLED UP the calendar on his laptop and
his eye caught on the date it so often did lately
He'd simply marked it with a digital icon as
reminder. Next month was Clairey's birthday
He'd gathered that bit of knowledge out of he
by chance last week. Birthdays called for cele
brations. He would use that celebration to com
clean with her once and for all about finally ad
dressing the proverbial elephant in the room.

For months, ever since the night of the pre
miere, they'd been the utmost professionals
Which meant they'd tiptoed around each othe

Was it so wrong that they'd enjoyed each other'
company? And that kiss they'd shared—thing
between them had certainly turned awkward
afterward. He refused to allow himself to re
gret it. It may have started out for the sheikl
and sheikha's benefit. But it had quickly turne
to something much more. Her lips against his

he taste of her. He still thought about it every night, couldn't get it out of his mind.

Yes, she was his fiancée in name only. Realisically, she was Marnie's nanny. But she was so much more than that. Both to him and Marnie. It was about time one of them acknowledged that fact. Being in his employ, Clairey was probably hesitant to broach the subject. Plus, he struck her as simply shy at times.

So it was up to him. They were both adults. Adults didn't ignore what was so blatantly obvious. And it was obvious the two of them had loads of chemistry. It was high time he did something about it. He'd take her out for her birthday to do just that.

He was pulled out his musings by the alert of an incoming call from his administrative assistant. He glanced at his watch. The woman lived on the West Coast and very rarely called him before noon.

Unless it was urgent.

He tapped to answer before the second ringone. "Drexel. There's a matter of concern you should know about. There's been a gentleman who's been calling for weeks now. I think you need to talk to him."

Drexel's mouth went dry as he listened to the rest of what she had to say. In less than two minutes, he'd heard enough to have alarm bells sounding loudly in his head.

"I can try and get him on the line now," Alyss offered.

As much as he wanted to avoid the conversation that would ensue, Drexel had never been one to put off the inevitable, no matter how unpleasant. And this was definitely going to be unpleasant.

"Put him through."

"Mr. Osoman, my name is Bill Thomas."

"What can I do for you, Mr. Thomas?" Drexel asked, though by now he had a pretty clear idea. And even the thought of the possibility had ice running through his veins.

The other man sighed into the phone before he answered. "I believe my daughter had a relationship with your younger brother about seven years ago. I think there are some things we need to discuss."

Seven years ago. The daughter this man had just referred to would be Marnie's mother. He was speaking with his niece's maternal grandfather.

"What kinds of things?"

"We have some concerns about our granddaughter."

Drexel felt his hands clench at his sides. "And those concerns would be?"

"Mainly that she's living with her single uncle."

"I'm engaged to—"

The man was abrupt. "We've read all about it. You've taken up with the girl's nanny, it appears. None of the sites mention any kind of planned wedding or date. You've had plenty of relationships before that went nowhere. It's all out there in black and white. In fact, you were engaged once before, it seems."

The man had certainly done his research. He'd clearly come prepared for this call.

For the umpteenth time in his life, Drex cursed the tabloids that made such fodder of his life. His previous so-called engagement had been nothing but a publicity stunt for the actress he'd been dating at the time. She'd fed the rumors to countless gossip sites worldwide. They'd reported on the fake story relentlessly, plastered his picture with the starlet all over the internet. Drex had been too much of a gentleman to deny the misinformation. At the time, he couldn't be bothered: it all seemed so trivial. He regretted that now.

The other man continued. "Your lifestyle is not very stable, Mr. Osoman. I understand my granddaughter has already been displaced from one home with her other grandmother and again after staying with her father for a while."

"Be that as it may, she's settled now."

"I believe she'd be better off with us." That was certainly blunt.

Drexel listened with minimal restraint to

what the other man had to say, offering little in return.

"We are her blood, Mr. Osoman," he finally finished.

Somehow, Drexel kept himself in check and managed not to laugh out loud at that statement. As if blood was enough to ensure love and security. What mattered was love and affection and respect. Marnie had all that and more here in New York with him and Clairey.

He'd heard enough. "I'll be in touch, Mr. Thomas," he said, then ended the call without waiting for a response.

Suddenly, all his plans for the next few weeks, including ones about Clairey, had to be relegated to secondary importance. All the pressing work projects would have to wait, as well. Thank heavens the sheikh had finally signed on all the necessary dotted lines.

His one focus now was to do well by his niece. Without any doubt, Marnie's best interest was to remain exactly where she was. With him and Clairey.

As soon as Drexel hung up, he made another call. This one to his personal attorney.

It was time for a serious conversation. She had to do it before Marnie got home. Marnie never allowed Clairey to say a cross word to any of these three. She approached the three felines,

Georgie, Porgie, and Pumpkin Pie as they swatted around their scratching post.

"Which one of you knocked over all the plants? Or was it all of you?" she asked.

Six bright green eyes blinked at her before ignoring her completely and returning to their batting and clawing. She waved a finger in the air to all of them and none of them in particular. "Don't let me catch you doing it again. You made a horrible mess on the carpet. It took me forever to clean it up."

That was a slight exaggeration. But the cats didn't need to know that. Clairey had to chuckle at herself and the picture she must make. At the ripe old age of twenty-six, she'd somehow become a cat lady. And they weren't even her pets!

Drexel chose that moment to fling the door of his study open and stride over to where she stood reprimanding the heedless cats. Whoa. After all these months, the sight of the man still took her breath away. He was dressed in his usual work uniform of silk shirt, baby-blue today, and pressed tailored dark pants. He was due for a haircut soon, but it had been a particularly busy month so his dark hair fell in soft waves over his forehead. Her fingers itched to run her fingers through it. She longed to feel his lips on hers again.

But she'd never gotten the courage to ask the way she had the night of the raffle. They were both doing a spectacular job of pretending they'd never kissed at all. Not the night of the auction. And not during the movie premiere.

It couldn't go on. Sooner or later, something had to give. But she hadn't found a way to ask the questions that plagued her. Had either of their kisses meant anything to him? The night of the premiere, when he'd touched her and caressed and softly brushed his lips against hers, was all that solely for the benefit of the sheikh? Could there possibly have been anything more to any of it?

Would she ever find a way to get any answers from him?

But all those thoughts fled her mind when she got a good look at his expression. The look he wore on his face had Clairey's pulse quickening. Something was very, very wrong.

"What is it?"

"Marnie's still at school?"

She nodded. "For hours still. And she'll be even later today. There's a rehearsal for the fall play."

"Good. It will give us a chance to talk. Do you have a minute?"

"Of course." She followed him into the sitting area.

Though he motioned for her to sit, Drexel continued standing and pacing. She'd never seen him so agitated. It took all her will not to jump

p, give him a good shake and demand that he
ll her what was happening already.

"I got a rather unwelcome phone call earlier
day," he finally began.

"Oh, no. Was it about your mother? Is she
kay?"

He blinked at her as if confused. "No. I speak
ith her doctors twice a week. And I was just
ere to visit her the other day, as you know.
here's been no change in her condition."

That was a relief, at least. "Then, what is it?"

"The phone call was about Marnie."

Clairey's heart began to thud in her chest.
What about her?" A horrifying possibility
me to her. "Was it her father?" She couldn't
ing herself to voice more of her fears.

"No. Not her father. Not Chase."

"Then, who?"

Drexel finally sat down. With clear weari-
:ss, he braced his forearms on his knees and
ared at the floor.

Okay. Now she was starting to get a little
ooked.

"Marnie's maternal grandparents only recently
und out about her. They've been estranged
om their daughter due to the woman's addic-
n issues. By chance they came upon one of
:r friends who happened to let it slip that their
ughter had had a child about six years ago."

Clairey could hardly hear him over the pounding in her ears. She knew where this conversation was headed.

Drexel continued. "They've been trying to locate her ever since. Apparently, a family friend of theirs who happens to be a retired police detective finally managed to do just that about three weeks ago."

She swallowed past the brick that had suddenly lodged itself in her throat. "Maybe it's not so bad. Maybe they just want to visit the granddaughter they've never seen."

He shook his head with a sadness she'd never seen him display before. "They don't just want to visit her, Clairey. They think it's in Marnie's best interest to have her live with them. Permanently."

Clairey's mouth went dry. "Oh, no. They can't truly mean that. Did you explain to them how much she's thriving here? Her school, her friends, the city she's grown to love?" Not to mention the guardian uncle who clearly loves her and dotes on her? She didn't say that last part aloud, however.

"I could tell there was no use. On the contrary, he said he was concerned about his granddaughter living with a known bachelor who's been linked to several high-profile women and has been photographed more than once at various parties."

"But that's just not true. The only parties you attend are for charity or work events."

"He didn't seem to think that matters. I'm technically a bachelor, and he can offer her a steady home with her grandmother and grandfather. That's the argument they plan to make if any of this gets to court, anyway."

"Did you tell them you were engaged?"

He nodded. "He doesn't seem to care. Thinks it doesn't mean much, given my past liaisons."

Clairey chose to ignore the pang that particular phrasing caused in her chest. Her panic was slowly beginning to turn to ire. These grandparents had no idea what they were doing. Marnie was happy here. She had everything a little girl could want. Including an uncle who loved her like any father would. And Clairey loved her too. She'd come to that realization without any kind of big revelations. It was just the truth that became more and more obvious with each passing day. To take Marnie away from all that would be heartless.

"I can't bear to think of her being uprooted yet again," Drexel said, echoing her thoughts.

"Maybe we can compromise with them. They can have her over the summers. That way she'll get to know her grandparents and not give up her life here."

"All options are on the table. I spoke with my attorney immediately afterward," Drexel said.

"Of course, he's going to do what he can fro[m]
a legal standpoint, file all the necessary pape[r]
work. But he had some guidance as a frien[d]
also."

"What kind of guidance?"

"He thinks there's a card I might be able [to]
play. A rather unconventional one. There mig[ht]
be a way to stave off the threat of any kind [of]
custody battle. You might be able to help m[e]
to do that."

For the first time since Drexel had mention[ed]
the phone call, Clairey felt a ray of hope. "Wh[at]
is it? What can we do?"

"I know how much this will be asking of yo[u,]
Clairey. But I have to ask."

"Ask what exactly?"

He took her hand, held her gaze. "No mo[re]
pretending. I'm asking you to marry me. It h[as]
to be real. You would have to be my real wif[e.]
In every way that counts."

Clairey stared at him as if he'd just spoken [a]
foreign language. Maybe he shouldn't hav[e]
blurted it out that way. But he'd never been o[ne]
to beat around the bush. She gave her head [a]
brisk shake.

"I'm sorry," she chuckled into her palm. "[I]
must be hearing things. It almost sounded li[ke]
you just proposed. To me."

"That's exactly what I did. Our best hope

keep Marnie here where she belongs is for us to get married."

He'd rendered her speechless. Not that he could blame her.

"Think about it. Their biggest argument is that Marnie is living with a bachelor uncle with no roots. We could counter that with the image of a family, including an adopting mother who happened to have been taking care of her for the past several months."

She sat motionless on the sofa. "I see."

"It wouldn't be a real marriage, Clairey." Was it his imagination or did she just flinch ever so slightly? He continued. "We're just doing this for appearances. To give Marnie the best chance possible to stay with us. As her guardians."

She remained silent, wringing her hands and staring at the carpet between her bare toes. If she didn't say something soon, Drexel thought he might very well lose his mind. Or his nerve.

But he couldn't do that. There really were no other options. He carried on in an attempt to fill the silence. "In the meantime, we have to be seen doing things that engaged couples do."

She looked up at him then, slight panic in her eyes. "Like what?"

He shrugged. "Spend time together. Both as a couple and as a family with Marnie."

"Seen by who, exactly?"

"The people who mostly pay attention to such

things. New York–society gossip pages. Websites and rags that depend on prying into others' lives for sales and clicks."

She visibly swallowed. "We're going to be the subject of sales and clicks?"

He moved from his position to sit next to her. Gave her a playful bump on the shoulder with his own. "Just for a little while. They'll lose interest soon enough. By then, we'll have gotten plenty of photos that prove how much in love we are."

Her head snapped up as he said the one loaded word. "Come on," he said, teasing. "You can pretend you love me for a while, can't you?"

She ignored the question.

He pressed on. "Of course, you'd be compensated. I don't expect you to go through all this for nothing."

Her head snapped up again, anger clear in her eyes. "You don't have to bribe me, Drexel. If I do this, I'd be doing it for Marnie. Not for some monetary reward."

Great. Now he'd made her mad. She'd gone from confused to angry in the blink of an eye because he'd mentioned payment. Maybe that was crass. But what did she expect from him? He was flying blind here. He'd never faced the prospect of having to fight for custody of a child before.

"I'm sorry," he told her sincerely.

This time, she was the one to nudge his shoulder. "Apology accepted."

"Of course, you'd be doing this for Marnie's sake."

But just as much for him.

She'd asked if she could sleep on it. Which was laughable, really. As if she'd be able to get any sleep. Clairey tossed over to her other side on the mattress yet again.

Up until now they'd simply been pretending. Now, Drex wanted to make it legal. A fake engagement was one thing. But a true marriage on paper was a whole other ball game.

What would it mean for her to go through with it? More importantly, what would it mean for her heart? The idea of a real marriage wouldn't have even occurred to Drexel if it wasn't for that blasted phone call he'd received from Marnie's grandfather. And if that fact left a small hole in her heart, well then, that was her problem.

For Marnie. She'd be doing this for Marnie. When she thought about the impact her decision would have on the little girl, Clairey really had no choice. She had been fooling herself to think she might possibly turn him down.

She would do it. She would accept Drexel's sham marriage proposal. Even though her heart was going to slowly shatter at how fake it all was. When she yearned to have it be real, somehow.

With her decision made, sleep finally began tugging at her, and she managed to drift off.

The dream came sometime toward dawn. In it, she wore a long white bridal gown of the finest lace. A bouquet of pink roses graced her hands. With excitement and anticipation, she slowly walked down the aisle. But when she reached the altar, there was no one there waiting for her. No groom to meet her. The bouquet fell out of her hands, the once-fresh roses now wilted and dry.

She was alone.

Clairey woke with a start. It was no use. She had no hope of getting back to sleep. Crawling out of bed, she went to make some much-needed coffee.

Apparently, she wasn't the only one plagued with insomnia. Drexel was already at the counter, impatiently drumming his fingers as he waited for his own coffee to brew.

He tossed an expectant look her way when he noticed her entrance.

"I'll do it, Drexel. I'll be your fake wife."

His features flushed with relief, and he tilted his head back, releasing a deep sigh.

A twinge of guilt nudged her chest at his reaction. He'd really been worried she might say no. Now that she was sure, Clairey realized she'd ever even really considered the alternative. Her mind had just needed the time to process it all.

Drexel leveled a loaded gaze at her. "Thank you, Clairey. Someday Marnie will understand just how much you're doing for her."

She pulled out a stool and sat while Drexel prepared a cup for her. By now, he knew exactly how she preferred her morning latte. "As long as it works."

"It has to. There's no plan B."

"So how exactly do we start?"

He set her cup down on the counter and slid with precision into her waiting hands.

"Thank you," she said and took an appreciative sip.

"You said Marnie's at school for a few hours later today at rehearsal again, right?"

"That's right."

"That leaves us free to set some of this in motion." He pulled out his own stool and sat down next to her. "I figured we'd start with brunch."

It couldn't be that simple, could it? "That's it? We're going to be a couple who do brunch? That's how we'll convince people?"

He winked at her. "You'll see."

He was right. Four hours later, Clairey had the answer to her question. The brunch Drexel had planned for them involved a 1920s luxury yacht set to sail along New York Harbor. The menu included seafood omelets, truffle pancakes and bubbly mandarin juice mimosas. There were about seven other couples onboard.

"This is quite the excursion," she commented as they took their seats. Servers immediately appeared at their table with crystal flutes full of the cocktail and trays of steaming, mouth-watering food.

"That's the financial district," Drexel told her as they sailed past a square of tall buildings and steel structures. Minutes later, in the distance to her left, Clairey could see the Statue of Liberty standing majestically over the wavy water.

"I never thought one could see so much of New York via boat." But Drexel wasn't listening. Without warning, he ran the back of his hand down Clairey's cheek and leaned close to plant a soft kiss along the base of her neck. She couldn't help the shiver that ran down from her spine clear to her toes. How often had she relived their kisses?

Then she realized what was happening. One of the other couples sat across the hull, their food completely ignored. The man had a cell phone aimed square in their direction.

"I believe they're from *Billionaire* magazine." Drexel said softly so that only she could hear though he made it appear as if he was whispering sweet nothings in her ear.

"There's something called *Billionaire* magazine?"

He nodded at her. "Yup. They have a ranking system and everything. I was at the top once or twice."

She didn't find that hard to believe. "How did they know you'd be here?"

"An anonymous tip strategically placed to various outlets."

Wow. He really wasn't leaving any of this to chance. Proving her point, he leaned over and dropped another kiss, this time closer to her lips. He was certainly putting on a show. All the while, heat suffused her body, and longing surged through her core. She had to get a grip. Yet again, none of this was real. Drexel was here for one reason and one reason only. It was the only reason he was touching her, caressing her, just like that night back in the theater.

She'd be a fool to forget that. Even if his fake kisses were having a very real effect on her soul.

How many times could she make the same mistake, anyway?

CHAPTER THIRTEEN

IT WAS A beautiful day for a wedding.

Clairey stared out her suite window at th
bright shining sun as it rose above the Manha
tan skyline. By this time tomorrow, she'd be
married woman.

On paper, anyway.

In every other way, she suspected her li!
would pretty much continue as it was. Asid
from the four-karat diamond on a plain gol
band on her finger, there'd be nothing differe
about her. She'd still essentially be the nann
Drexel employed. Not really his wife in any wa
that meant anything.

A soft knock on her door pulled her out (
her thoughts.

She released a pent-up sigh and turned awa
from the view to answer. Tessa was early, it a
peared. She was due in an hour to help her g
ready for the big day. Maybe Tessa had caugl
an earlier flight. Lana would be helping her t
get ready too. Her bridesmaids. They were bo

beyond excited for her. Clairey still hadn't decided how much of the truth she would tell her two friends. For now, they believed that she and Drexel were tying the knot for all the right reasons. Though, they couldn't figure out why the two of them were rushing the wedding.

But it wasn't Tessa standing outside her door when she opened it. Drexel stood there with his arm braced against the doorframe.

"Oh, it's you." Even now, she felt the tingle of thrill that she experienced every time she laid eyes on the man. In as drab an outfit as a cotton T-shirt and loose sweatpants, he somehow still managed to exude pure masculine sex appeal.

"Can I come in?"

She stepped aside and motioned for him to enter.

"I know it's supposed to be taboo to see the bride before the wedding," he said, brushing past her. "But I figured in our case, the usual superstitions don't apply. And not on the day before."

Because none of it was real. "I think that mostly refers to the bride in her wedding gown, anyway," she said, turning to face him.

He reached inside his pants pocket to pull out a long rectangular box. Clairey immediately recognized the logo on the top cover. The designer boutique on the Cape.

"I've been meaning to give this to you ever

since that day. There never seemed to be a good time."

She reached for the box and opened it. Inside resting among soft velvet fabric sat a glittering glass necklace. One of the two she'd watched him purchase that day.

"I figured this was as good a time as any."

She blinked up at him, confused. "I thought you got this for Marnie."

He shook his head. "No, I bought it for you. It was always meant for you."

Clairey felt touched beyond words. Even back then he'd been thinking of her enough to get her something sentimental. "I... Thank you."

"I debated that day about the appropriateness of getting you a gift. We'd just met, after all. So I held onto it."

"Until today."

"I figured the flower girl and the bride could wear matching necklaces."

She pulled the piece of jewelry out of the box and admired it. The way it caught the sunlight from the window, the beauty of the design. "May I?" Drexel asked.

She handed it to him, and he gently unclasped the small gold fastener. Then he stepped behind her. His fingers felt warm and firm against her skin. A current of heat traveled down her neck to her center as he put the necklace on her. Was it her imagination, or did his hands linger along her neck a moment or two longer after he'd fastened the clasp?

"It's beautiful," Clairey told him when he was done, fingering the delicate glass. "Thank you."

He'd have no idea just how much the gift meant to her. When he'd given her the diamond for their fake engagement, she'd known how unreal it was. That ring was only for show, pretense.

This felt so much more genuine. Ceremonial. Drex had gotten this necklace especially for her. The sentiment made a world of difference.

Their upcoming wedding might be a farce, as was their pretend engagement. But as far as Clairey was concerned, this moment was genuine.

And so were her feelings for her soon-to-be so-called husband.

He hadn't expected to feel quite so nervous. None of this was real, after all. They just had to go through this sham of a ceremony so that the gossip sites would do their write-ups and publish a few photos and he would have concrete proof that he was a married man.

Nothing in his life was about to change in any real way. Except that, technically, he'd have a wife. That wife being Clairey.

On paper, anyway.

Things had been so different between them

the last time they'd been on this rooftop the night of the school raffle. She'd fallen asleep in his arms on a chaise longue. They'd woken up to see the sunrise the next morning. He would have never guessed that night that in a few months' time he'd be waiting for her at a makeshift altar for an impromptu wedding.

The ding of the elevator signaled her arrival. Clairey exited the doors soon after.

Drexel's breath caught in his throat at the sight of her. Even through the veil and from this distance, she was heart-stoppingly beautiful. A vision. There was no other way to describe her in her wedding gown. It complemented her figure and hugged her curves in a way that made him imagine taking it off her later. He pushed that thought aside.

Marnie walked slowly in front of her, dropping delicate rose petals along the aisle. Clairey's two friends flanked her as bridesmaids and in lieu of the father she'd lost who would have given her away.

Drexel couldn't tear his eyes away from her as she made her way down the runner. He had to remind himself this wasn't any kind of authentic wedding. They'd rushed the ceremony and just needed to get it over with.

So why was there a rush of emotion surging through him at the moment?

Clairey reached his side and gave him a small

nile through her veil. Her brown hair a dark
ontrast against the white fabric, adding to the
riking allure of the overall picture she made.
The officiant began speaking, but his words
arely registered. Not until Drexel heard him
y, "You may kiss your bride."

e hadn't so much as touched her since the
edding. Now, over a week later, Drexel was
olding her hand. Only because they were in
very public place. He was only doing it for
ow. Their little charade continued now that
ey were among others. Behind closed doors,
owever, nothing had really changed between
em. They still kept their separate living quar-
rs. Drexel hadn't invited her into his suite even
nce.

Clairey tried not to let the hurt of that ruin
er mood as they took their seats in the school's
iditorium. Marnie could barely contain her ex-
tement this morning about her role as a small
ourd in the Hammond School's autumn perfor-
ance of "Harvest Moon," a play written by the
ildren themselves. So far, the little girl was
rprisingly oblivious to the dynamics in her
ousehold. Clairey had to wonder if she found
odd that her uncle and nanny were currently
asband and wife, yet they behaved exactly as
fore with each other.

Drexel gave her hand a squeeze and pulled

it over onto his lap. Her pulse quickened at the rather intimate action. Funny, no one was watching them now. In fact, the lights had dimmed. There was no need to put on such a display. Still, he made no move to let go of her. Probably just a reflexive action at this point. Clairey decided not to question it. A girl could get used to such tender gestures, regardless of motive.

Moments later, the curtains drew open to reveal several children on stage dressed as fall vegetables in colorful costumes. The first act did not go smoothly. All the children flubbed their lines, earning amused laughs from the audience. One little redheaded boy completely forgot what he was to say and stood frozen until the teacher walked onto the stage to help him out. Marnie, for her part, only missed a word here and there. Her bright smile told Clairey she was enjoying herself.

At the end of the performance, the little thespians received a standing ovation. Drexel seemed to be clapping louder and more enthusiastically than most anyone else. He even blew out a loud whistle when Marnie took her bow.

"I'll admit, I enjoyed that more than I thought I would," he said when the curtains were drawn and the houselights came on. Marnie came running out from backstage moments later.

Drexel lifted the girl in his arms and twirled

her once. "There she is. You were a star up there, sweetheart."

Marnie giggled. "Silly Uncle Drex. I was a baby pumpkin."

"The best baby pumpkin to ever grace the stage."

Drexel put her back down, and Marnie immediately ran over to give Clairey a tight hug around the waist. "You were the best pumpkin I've ever seen."

A ringtone sounded from Drexel's pocket. She heard him utter a soft curse as he pulled out his phone and glanced at the screen.

"Excuse me, ladies. I need to take this call."

Marnie gave her one more tight squeeze around the middle before dropping her arms and jumping in place.

Clairey had to laugh at her exuberance. "You are so excited, little one."

"I'm gonna go back to my friends now. We're making sundaes to celebrate our great show." With that, she ran back to her teacher and group of classmates.

Clairey found Drexel in the hallway just as he ended the call. The dark expression on his face told her the conversation had not been a pleasant one.

"Where's Marnie?" he asked, looking behind her for the little girl.

"Off with the rest of her class. They're having

an ice-cream party back in their classroom. W
can pick her up in a couple of hours."

She pointed to the cell phone in his han
"What was the call about?"

"That was my attorney," he told her, repoc
eting the phone.

An icy dread washed through her veins. Th
call had to be about Marnie. "The Thomase
have requested a visit. They're planning on fl
ing into New York within the next week. The
want to meet Marnie and see for themselves h
exact living situation."

She reached for him without thinking. "W
have to let them, Drexel. And we'll just have
deal with whatever the fallout may be."

He released a heavy sigh and crammed h
fingers into the hair at his crown. "I know.
can't keep her grandparents from her con
pletely. She has a right to know who they are

"I couldn't agree more. I would have give
anything to have a set of grandparents aroun
after losing my father. But they were all gone b
the time I was born." Clairey knew this wasn
about her. But having two other people in th
world who cared for her might have made
mountain of difference in the lonely way she
had to live her life. No matter the older couple
intentions, Clairey knew the meeting was inev
table. She was surprised they hadn't made th
request before.

"I'm glad you're being reasonable about this. We have to think of what's best for Marnie when we make these decisions."

He nodded, and a darkness settled over his eyes she'd never seen before. Clairey got the feeling she was getting her first glimpse of the self-made successful businessman who went after what he wanted and made sure to get it. His words when he answered served to confirm that thought.

"I can be reasonable, Clairey. But only to a degree," Drexel said between gritted teeth. "Grandparents or not, I know Marnie's better off with us."

She couldn't argue that, thinking of how happy Marnie had been up on that stage and of her excitement about having ice cream with all her new friends.

Drexel continued, "I'll fight them with all I have if they try to take her."

The Thomases looked like they could be models for a cooking-magazine photo spread. Or in a Norman Rockwell painting. Muriel Thomas had bluish-gray hair she wore in tight curls. Dressed in a smart cream-colored knee-length skirt and flat loafers, she gave every impression of the cookie-baking, Sunday-roast-preparing, matronly grandma. Bill Thomas had lost most of his hair. He had wide shoulders and large hands that had clearly helped him make his living.

Drexel had led them into the living room when they'd arrived two minutes ago. They were waiting for Clairey to go get Marnie from her room. "My wife will be right out with Marnie. She's just finishing getting dressed."

Bill gave him a suspicious look. "Wife, huh?"

Drexel lifted an eyebrow in question. "Something you'd like to get off your chest, Mr. Thomas?"

Muriel placed a cautionary hand on her husband's forearm, but the man ignored it.

"I just think it's mighty convenient how you happened to get married sometime after our first phone call." Apparently, Bill wasn't one to pull any punches.

It took plenty of restraint, but Drexel somehow managed to clamp down on his ire. These people may have Marnie's best interest at heart, but so far, he was less than pleased with their approach.

Clairey entered the room at that moment with Marnie practically clinging to her leg. The girl was nervous. Drexel could hardly blame her. Two strangers she'd never seen before had made a trip from halfway across the country to visit her. It didn't help that Marnie knew nothing of her mother, let alone the type of people her maternal grandparents might be.

Clairey rubbed the top of Marnie's head in reassurance. "Marnie. This is your grandmother and grandfather."

Not for the first time, Drexel said a silent prayer of thanks that Clairey was here to help him through this. He'd faced countless adversaries both on the streets as a teenager and in the boardroom. But he was certain he'd be handling all this much more poorly if it wasn't for her support and understanding. Not to mention her presence now.

He needed to keep his wits about him. And he needed to stay calm and even-keeled. With Clairey's help, he just might be able to.

"Would you like to go say hello?"

Marnie hesitantly let go of Clairey's leg and took a small bow. "Hello. I'm Marnie."

Muriel clasped a hand to her chest and let out a small cry. "Oh, my. She's utterly precious. Becky looked so much like her as a little girl." Her eyes suddenly flooded with tears before she turned away and pulled a tissue out of her purse.

Marnie looked up at Clairey in question. Clairey gave her a reassuring smile and a gentle nudge. Drexel felt a tug in his chest at the picture the two of them made. The Thomases had to see what he was seeing. In the previous months, Clairey had been more of a mother to Marnie than anyone else in the girl's short life so far. They'd have to be blind to miss that even in the brief time they'd been here.

Marnie finally dropped Clairey's hand and walked over to stand between the older couple on the couch.

"May I hug you?" Muriel asked.

Marnie nodded her answer. Drexel watched as the two embraced. Then Bill joined in and put his large, burly arms around the two of them.

A slew of conflicting thoughts rushed through his head. Marnie's grandparents were clearly affectionate and caring people. They were already showing how much love they'd bestow on their grandchild. The scene before him was genuine and heartfelt, there was no doubt.

Drexel tore his eyes away from the three of them and made his way to where Clairey stood. Her eyes had grown rather misty, as well. Without hesitation or thought, he pulled her tight up against him and held her against his length. The scent of her calmed him. She felt like a steadying anchor to his storm of conflicting emotions.

He needed her more than he knew. And it had somehow happened when he hadn't even been paying attention.

A week later, after half a dozen more visits between Marnie and her grandparents, Bill Thomas rang from the lobby asking to meet with Drexel. When the man arrived at his of-

ice, he had a look of resignation on his face.
'et, Drexel could read something else in his
xpression as well. Relief.

"I'm going to be honest with you, Mr. Oso-
1an."

"Please call me Drexel."

The other man nodded. "Drexel. My wife isn't
1 the best of health. She's fighting a recurrence
f a battle we thought she'd won long ago."

"I'm very sorry to hear that."

"But we had to make sure our grandchild was
ll right."

Why couldn't he have just said all that from
1e get-go? It could have saved everyone so
1uch angst and worry. Drexel kept the thought
> himself.

"We had to see for ourselves," Bill added.
Bad enough we lost our daughter to her ad-
ictions, we couldn't not know our grandchild."

"I understand."

Bill scratched at his head. "I think we've seen
nd heard enough. I'll admit to speculating on
our sudden marriage. But the end result for
1arnie seems to be a well-adjusted household
here she's well taken care of. It's all we wanted
> know."

"Thank you for that."

"Our only ask is that we can come visit her.
.nd maybe have her come stay with us and
1eet some of her cousins."

Drexel made sure not to react in any kind o celebratory way. The whole dilemma was work ing out the way he'd hoped. But he couldn't fee any satisfaction at the struggles these two peo ple were dealing with. "You're welcome her whenever you'd like," he assured the other man "You and your wife and any cousins who migh want to make the trip. In fact, the flight an lodgings are on me."

Bill immediately shook his head. "We don accept any kind of charity."

Drexel held a hand up to stop him from say ing any more. "It wouldn't be charity. I'd b doing it for my niece. The more people she ha in her life who love her, the better for her."

Bill rubbed his jaw. "Well, in that case, I'l take it up with the wife."

They shook hands on it before Bill turned t leave. Drexel watched the door shut behind th other man and gave in to the surge of relief tha flooded through every cell in his body.

He wouldn't celebrate alone. After all, ther was one other person who shared this victor with him. Clairey. His wife.

CHAPTER FOURTEEN

"So, TO WHAT do I owe this honor, big brother?" Chase sat across from him sipping the fine brandy he'd taken upon himself to order along with his dinner. Drexel figured it was a small price to pay if this little get-together accomplished what he intended.

Chase continued after several more sips. "Did you invite me here and fly me in for a belated bachelor party or something?"

Drex took a moment to study his only sibling. Chase's cheeks were ruddy, his eyes slightly bloodshot. He'd guess the glass he held wasn't his first one of the day. "Not exactly," he answered.

"Then, why am I here? I've left my wife all the way back in Maine to come. We're still technically newlyweds, you know. Though, not as new as you and what's-her-name."

Drexel somehow held onto his temper, although it wasn't easy. "Her name is Clairey. Clairey Osoman now." He wouldn't bother to

ask Chase if he wanted to see Marnie. It hadn
even occurred to his brother to ask about hi
only child.

Chase held his glass in the air in a mock toas
"Ah, yes. Clairey. How did you two come abou
getting married again? Didn't you just meet th
woman a short while ago when she tried to de
stroy my wedding?"

He would ignore the jab. Never mind tha
Clairey had been absolutely right to try and in
tervene. He shuddered to think of the life Ma
nie might be subjected to now if Clairey hadn
stormed into the meeting room that morning.

Remarkable, really, the impact she'd had o
his life since then. Somehow, when he hadn
been looking or paying attention, she'd becom
a true partner. A support and anchor he hadn
even known he'd needed. Or wanted.

A small twinge of apprehension itched in h
chest at those thoughts, but he didn't have tim
to examine that right now.

He answered his brother, steepling his finge
over the table. "We've grown quite fond of eac
other since then." Best to just get this over wit
"Marnie's quite fond of her, as well. They're
Central Park right now enjoying Shakespea
in the Park."

Chase cut into his steak, took a bite an
chewed. "What's any of that got to do with wh
I'm here?"

"There's some paperwork I'd like you to sign."

Chase may as well have rolled his eyes, his boredom was so clear. "What kind of paperwork?"

"I got a phone call a few weeks ago. From Marnie's maternal grandparents."

That seemed to get his attention. "Oh? What'd they want?"

"Mainly to meet Marnie. But they were also concerned."

Chase set down his knife and fork and leaned back in his chair. "About what, exactly?"

"They were thinking about having Marnie live with them until they saw how well she's taken to her life here."

"Huh."

"I don't want to risk something like that happening again."

Chase had to know what he was thinking. Now that Marnie's grandparents were appeased, the only one who still posed any kind of threat that his niece might be taken away from Drex and Clairey was sitting across the table.

"It might have gone differently if it wasn't for Clairey. We might have lost Marnie to her grandparents."

Chase tilted his head to the side. "Yeah?" His brother may have been reckless and lazy, but he'd never been stupid. Chase put the pieces together almost immediately. A knowing smirk formed along his lips. "That explains it. It's why you married her, isn't it?"

Drexel didn't bother to try to deny it. It wasn't as if Chase's thoughts on his marriage meant anything to him. That wasn't the kind of brothers they were, and it wasn't what this meeting was about.

He got right to the point. "I want you to sign over custody. I'd like to begin the process of adopting Marnie. It will go much more smoothly if done with your cooperation."

Chase took another sip of his drink. "Why would I do that?"

He had to ask? Drexel took a steadying breath. He wasn't going to let his brother goad him into losing his composure. "Because you don't want to be a father. Not to Marnie, anyway."

"I might change my mind about that at some point in the future."

"And what would happen if you do change your mind? You would pluck her from the life she's grown into and take her away from all that she loves?"

"I'm her father."

He'd hardly acted like it. "You'll always be part of her life. But I think it's in her best interest for Clairey and me to adopt her."

"You wanna adopt my kid? With your fake wife?"

Drexel clenched his fists under the table. Chase didn't give him a chance to respond before continuing. "You're a real piece of work, big brother."

"What's that supposed to mean?"

He leaned forward and drained the rest of his drink, motioned for a refill to the bartender across the dining room. "It means you always thought you were better than us. But the truth is you're not so different than the old man."

The blood pounded in his ears at the unwarranted accusation. Chase had some nerve. "I'm nothing like him. I never had to have a teenager come drag me away from the slot machines in the middle of the night. I never got beaten to a pulp because I cheated the wrong man at an underground card game. And I never lost money over and over again only to gamble more away the next day. Losing money that could have gone to feeding my impoverished family and keeping my sons off the streets."

Chase's eyes narrowed on him. "Maybe not. Or maybe you're just better at winning than he was."

"You're not making any sense."

"Face it, bro. The games might not be the same. But you do whatever it takes to win when you play. Like how you conned a young woman into a loveless marriage just so you could win yet again."

Drexel saw red as his brother's words echoed through his head. Chase didn't know what he was talking about. He'd married Clairey for his niece's sake. Not for some ego-driven desire to succeed or to best anyone else.

And he certainly didn't have to explain himself to anyone about it.

"You know what?" Chase bit out, pushing away from the table and crossing his arms over his chest. "Sure, I'll sign. But there's a price."

You can do this.

Clairey gave herself the same pep talk she'd been repeating since she'd woken up this morning. Sometime over the course of the past several days she'd come to a gradual realization. She was tired of waiting for Drexel to make the first move. Or any kind of move, for that matter.

As anxiety inducing as the Thomases' visit had been, it had led to Clairey reaching a profound conclusion. She wanted that kind of relationship for herself. Bill and Muriel had grown old together, faced hardships together, and were now surrounded by loving family and grandchildren they adored.

They'd been true partners in their marriage. Unlike the selfish love that Clairey had witessed between her mom and Frank, what the Thomases had was enviable to witness.

If there was even a chance that she might be able to achieve that with Drex, she would never forgive herself if she didn't take the chance to find out.

She was in love with him. There was no denying it any longer. And she wanted her marriage to be a real one. In every possible way.

No, Clairey had no idea what the future held for them. But right now, she wanted the type of intimacy that true couples shared. With the only man she'd ever fallen in love with.

He had to want this too. She could feel it in her bones. In the looks he gave her when he thought she wasn't watching. The way he touched her fingers in the mornings as he handed her the latte he'd prepared. The way his face lit up when he walked in and found her waiting for him in the kitchen. All that had to mean something.

Maybe she was about to make a fool of herself. Maybe all of this was simply wishful thinking. But one way or another, she was going to find out for certain if Drexel wanted her the same way she wanted him. As his authentic, legitimate wife in every way. Their union might have started as a means to an end. But tonight Clairey was going to try to make it a real marriage.

She wanted to make love to her husband.

Marnie was already at Sara's. Lana had agreed to take her for another sleepover. The silky red dress she'd purchased hung ready in the closet. She'd already done her hair.

The home-cooked meal she'd prepared simply needed to be popped in the oven when he came home.

Clairey had thought of everything.

But her plans hit a serious snag when two hours had gone by and Drexel still wasn't back. She glanced at her watch. It was already past nine. Where was he?

An hour later, panic was beginning to set in. Maybe there'd been some kind of emergency. Clairey's heart pounded against her chest as she reached for her phone on the glass coffee table. Straight to voice mail. A short text message went unanswered for another hour.

Just when she was deciding where to start trying to look for him, she heard the penthouse elevator ding.

Clairey scrambled off the couch to her feet and met him halfway in the kitchen. "You're home. I've been waiting for you."

He took one look at her and raised both eyebrows. Then his gaze traveled the length of her body, lingering at her plunging neckline. Clairey felt heat rise to her cheeks.

"Did we have plans? I didn't realize."

Hot tears sprang to her cheeks, but she refused to let him see. He hadn't realized because she'd taken great care to surprise him.

"Where have you been, Drex? I was worried sick."

He loosened his collar and undid several buttons on his shirt. Clairey wanted to kick herself for her reaction. Even now, given her distress, she wanted nothing more than to stride over to him and touch her fingers to the bronze skin at his chest. She wanted him to hold her, to tell her he was sorry for making her wait.

"You shouldn't have been worried. I just jumped into a quick round of cards at the gaming hall by the airport."

A card game? "I thought you hated those places."

His lips tightened. "Sorry you were worried, Clairey. But there's hardly need for all these questions. I just needed to blow off some steam after seeing Chase."

Of all the turns she might have expected this conversation to take, that had definitely not been on her radar. "Chase? You saw your brother?"

"Yes. I asked him to relinquish custody of Marnie to me."

Me. Not *us.* He was throwing her all sorts of curve balls. Clairey was having trouble processing.

"You didn't tell me."

"I didn't want to say anything until I was sur
Chase would sign."

"I see." But she didn't. Not really. She didn
see why he'd gone ahead and made such a hug
move without so much as mentioning it to he

"He signed."

Well, at least that was one less thing to worr
about. Marnie's future with them was secure
at least.

A bloom of hope blossomed in her chest
the thought. Maybe they had something to ce
ebrate tonight, after all.

But Drexel didn't appear celebratory. His e:
pression told her there was more he had to sa
Clairey's mouth went dry. She wasn't sure ho
much more she could take.

"There's something else, isn't there?"

He fingered his collar, clearly weighing h
words. "There's been a development with t
Abu Dhabi acquisition. It's going to require n
to give it my full attention."

"What kind of development?"

"There's been a lot of unexpected glitche
trying to break ground. I'll have to fly dow
there and stay until everything falls into plac
with the project. I took the liberty of calling
nanny service so that you'll have some help wi
Marnie while I'm overseas."

Okay. Yet another huge revelation. What
the world was happening right now? Clairey f

utterly unprepared. She somehow swallowed past the boulder that had lodged itself in the base of her throat. "When do you leave?"

"As soon as possible. Within the next twenty-four to forty-eight hours."

Clairey's stomach took a nosedive. A day or two? "How long will you be gone?"

"A year. Maybe more."

Her knees went weak as his words sank in. Despite his roundabout way of announcing it, she finally understood what was occurring right before her. He was leaving them. Leaving her. What a fool she'd been! While she was sitting here hoping to bring them closer together, he'd been setting all sorts of things into action that would do just the opposite.

"I know it's a lot to take in," he told her. "But it seemed to come together all at once."

If that wasn't the understatement of all time.

Drex made a move toward her but stopped himself. "Clairey? Say something."

What did he expect her to say even if she could make her mouth work? Finally, somehow, she found the words to sum up what she was hearing. "So you arranged to have me replaced as Marnie's primary caregiver, and you plan on moving thousands of miles away for the fore-seeable future. And you did it all without me having any kind of say in any of it. Do I have all that right?"

Clairey hated the tremble in her voice, hated the way she was shivering where she stood.

And she absolutely hated what Drexel had to say in response. "It's all for the best, Clairey."

Drexel shut the door of his suite and leaned up against the door with his eyes shut tight. A moment later, he heard the elevator door ping open then shut again.

She'd left the penthouse.

Go after her. Try to explain.

He reached for the doorknob to do just that before he stopped himself. There was no use. What was done was done. His brother's accusations had rattled him enough that he'd felt the need to test himself at the run-down casino by the airport near downtown. No, he hadn't enjoyed himself. Not even when he'd run the table and won. Thank goodness for that small assurance.

But that minor victory didn't make the rest of Chase's words any less relevant.

His brother was a thankless clod who'd just ransomed custody of his only child. But he'd also given voice to the misgivings that had plagued Drexel since he'd hired Clairey back on the Cape.

Her working for him was only supposed to have been temporary until the situation with Marnie was sorted and Clairey was back on her feet. Instead, he'd roped her into a sham marriage for his own needs.

Maybe with him gone and Marnie set up with a nanny service, Clairey would finally get a chance to pursue her own goals and go after her ambitions in life. He'd even make some calls, see what was out there for someone with her skills and experience. New York was the world's hub for tourism and hospitality, and Drexel had no doubt she would shine wherever she found herself. She might even meet somebody who deserved her for who she was and not simply as a way to use her for his own selfish needs. A stabbing pain shot through his midsection at the thought, but he had to ignore it.

As much as it pained him to walk away, he had no right to hold her back any longer.

CHAPTER FIFTEEN

"I TAKE IT your romantic evening didn't go as planned," Lana remarked upon opening the door to Clairey's knock. "The fuzzy socks and baggy sweatpants are a big clue if you're wondering how I know."

A hiccup of a sob escaped Clairey before she could stop it.

Her friend immediately stepped over the threshold and put her arms around her shoulders. "Oh, sweetie. Come in. Tell me what happened. Do I need to go over there with my heavy skillet?"

Clairey sniffled. "No. I mean, maybe. Maybe I need the skillet."

She followed Lana to the living room, and they both plopped down on the couch.

"The girls are engrossed in a movie they're streaming, and the Wallaces are at a dinner party. You have plenty of time to cry on my shoulder." She handed Clairey a full box of tissues.

Clairey hiccuped yet again and wanted to

.ick herself for it. She hated coming across so
veak, so wounded. But that's exactly how she
elt. Like she was about to lose something pre-
ious and coveted. Or she'd never had it in the
irst place.

"Tell me," Lana gently prompted.

Clairey struggled with how to start. Then she
imply blurted the whole story as best she could
elate—from Drexel showing up late to the fact
hat he'd been at a casino the whole time to all
he bombshells he'd dropped on her when he'd
inally turned up.

"Wow." Lana's vague response almost made
er chuckle. Almost. "That's a lot."

"He's leaving, Lana. Thousands of miles
way. For months on end."

Her friend tucked her legs under her on the
ofa cushion. "I'm missing something."

"What's that?"

"Well, for one, what did he say when you
old him everything you had planned? How you
anted to finally make it a true marriage?"

That gave her pause. Clairey stopped in the
ct of wiping her eyes to stare at her friend.
You knew?"

Lana shrugged. "I knew something was
miss. One day you two are employer and
anny, and the next you're engaged. Then sud-
enly you're rushing a wedding, just as Mar-

nie's grandparents show up. Something didn'
add up."

Great. Now she could feel guilty on top o
everything else. "I'm sorry I didn't tell you the
truth from the beginning."

Lana patted her knee. "That's a conversation
for another time. Now, tell me how he reacted
when you tried to seduce him."

Clairey cringed at the wording. Lana wa
right, though; there was no better way to de
scribe it.

"I never got the chance. I was so taken abacl
at all that was happening."

"Huh. So you have no idea how he migh
have reacted if your plans had come to fruition
tonight? If you'd told him exactly how you fee
about him?"

Clairey wrung the tissue in her hand so tigh
her knuckles began to hurt. "No, I don't." She
threw her hands up in frustration. "But wha
difference does it make?"

"I'd say it makes all the difference," Lana de
clared, handing her another tissue.

"He's leaving, Lana," she repeated. "He seem
very determined. And I don't think there's any
thing I can do to stop him."

"Oh, honey, aren't you even going to try?"

She wasn't back yet.

Drexel picked up his phone for the umpteent

time to call Clairey, only to toss it back in disgust. He had no idea what he would say to her when she answered. She might not even pick up. Which would be more than he deserved. Maybe it was better that she wasn't here. A clean break left fewer scars.

But he was going to slowly go crazy if he stayed up here in the penthouse any longer, rehashing the same pointless thoughts over and over. His half-hearted attempts to pack for Abu Dhabi were going nowhere and only added to his overall frustration. He couldn't even find his toiletry bag. And where the hell was his passport?

Drexel swore and tossed his bottle of aftershave so hard against the wall, a chip of paint fell to the floor. He rubbed a hand down his face and tried to calm down.

As happy as he was about the deal, being a huge business success, he knew he'd paid too much for the property. An impulsive move made on a whim due to his confusion and self-recrimination. Yet another gamble. Maybe his brother was right about him in more ways than one.

He had to get some air. A walk might do him some good, despite the late hour. Not bothering to grab any kind of jacket, he made his way down to the first floor.

Drexel did a double take when the elevator

doors slid open down in the lobby. A familia
figure stood over by the entrance. He rubbed hi
eyes to make certain he wasn't seeing things i
his agitated state. His eyes weren't tricking him

"Chase? What are you doing here?"

His brother shoved his fingers through hi
hair. "Working up the courage to come up an
try to see you."

"You were?" Drexel could guess the reason
Chase had no doubt rethought the amount he'
asked for earlier for Marnie's custody agree
ment. He was most likely here to renegotiat
what he'd already signed off on.

So be it. Drexel would write him anothe
large check. What his brother didn't understan
was that he'd have given him the money outrigh
merely for the asking. Custody or not.

"Got a minute to talk, big brother?" Chas
asked now, his hands jammed into his pocket

Drexel answered with a nod. "Walk with m
I was just going out to get some air."

The air was crisp and breezy when the
stepped onto the sidewalk and started walkin
in the direction of the park.

"Listen, man," Chase began, "our conversa
tion at the restaurant earlier didn't sit well wi
me."

That was unexpected. Drexel tried not to l
his surprise show and made sure to maintai
his steady stride.

Chase continued. "Look, I lashed out and said some things I knew better than to say."

This time Drexel did pause. He turned to face his brother. "Chase, are you actually trying to apologize?"

His brother gave him a chagrined smiled. "Well, duh. What do I have to do? Write you a card? Buy you flowers?"

"Huh," was the best Drexel could come up with in response.

Chase rolled his eyes and looked up at the sky. "All right, fine. I'll go ahead and say it all. We know you're better equipped to take care of Marnie. You're obviously more successful, you can offer her a better life. It's why I sent her off with you in the first place. I know I can't be a good father right now. But when confronted with the reality of all that, I let my insecurities get the best of me. And I took it out on you."

Drexel truly felt at a loss for words. Especially at his brother's next comments. "I know I have a lot to thank you for. You were the lifeline Mom and I never had with Dad. You were there to fix things whenever he broke them. Guess that's why I asked you to help me fix what went wrong with my daughter."

A ball of emotion welled up in his throat. To hear his brother say such things made him realize just how much he could use his own lifeline right about now. And how he'd pushed the one person away who was serving that very purpose.

Out of his own fear and insecurities. What a selfish fool he'd been.

His brother carried on. "I'm still trying to get my act together. We both know you make a better father than I do. And you're married to a woman who stuck up for Marnie when she didn't even know her. I know she'll help you take good care of her."

Drexel squeezed his eyes shut and bit out a curse.

"What is it?" Chase asked.

"I might have messed that up."

Chase narrowed his eyes on him. "Already? What'd you do?"

"I pushed her away." He wouldn't divulge the fact that he'd reacted as a direct result of taking everything Chase had said to him to heart. It wasn't as if he could lay the blame at Chase's feet. No one was responsible for his actions but himself.

Chase blew out a low whistle. "Well, you gotta fix it, man. 'Cause from the look on your face, I'd say you have no choice. That's the look of a man in love."

Drex exhaled a deep breath. Chase was right. It was so obvious: he'd fallen in love with Clairey. He just hadn't allowed himself to admit it. "I don't know if she'll forgive me."

"Guess there's only one way to find out, big brother. And you should get started—pronto."

Drexel couldn't help but huff out a small laugh. "How did you get so wise all of a sudden?"

A look of softness washed over his features. "Believe it or not, married life has been good for me. Danielle has been good for me. We have our individual issues we need to work on. But together we make a pretty good team."

Drexel gently cuffed his brother's shoulder. "I'm glad to hear that. Really."

"Besides, trust me. I have selfish reasons."

"Yeah, how so?"

"You can't let a woman like that get away," Chase said, waving a finger at him. "The way she made sure Marnie wasn't stuck where she wasn't wanted—only someone with a heart of gold and a boatload of courage would do something like that. And I'd want nothing less in a mother for my—" he caught himself and corrected the last word "—*our* little girl."

Drexel pulled him in a brotherly embrace.

Chase was right.

They had more in common as brothers than appeared on the surface. Just like Chase, Drexel had let his insecurities and doubts get in the way of his true shot at happiness. As a result, he just might have ruined the best thing that had ever come his way. The best chance he'd have at a life full of love.

He could only hope he wasn't too late.

Clairey awoke with a start and bolted up in bed. She hadn't even bothered to change into her night clothes or crawl under the covers. Drexel was gone again when she'd come back to the apartment last night. She'd fallen asleep waiting for him to return.

But she heard him now. In fact, two distinct voices could be heard coming from the hallway by the entrance elevator.

Clairey forced herself to take a fortifying breath and summoned all the strength she could. When she left her room, she found Drexel crouched in front of Marnie, speaking to her very intently.

He must have picked her up from Lana's earlier this morning.

Her stomach dropped when she realized why. He was saying goodbye to his niece. Several bags of luggage sat in front of the elevator doors. He certainly hadn't been kidding about leaving ASAP.

Drexel took Marnie's hand in his and must have asked her some kind of question as the little girl bobbed her head up and down in answer.

Clairey couldn't guess what they might be discussing, but Marnie clearly didn't understand

xactly what was happening or the gravity of
1e situation, for she appeared to be giggling
appily.

"You were gone late, last night," Clairey ven-
1red from her position several feet away from
here the two of them stood, afraid to get too
ose for fear of him seeing the sheen of tears
1 her eyes.

He straightened immediately upon hearing
1r voice. "Chase stopped by. We realized we
1d a lot of things left unsaid between us."

Another goodbye he'd gotten out of the way,
1en. She had to wonder if he'd planned on both-
ing to do so with her. A boulder of hurt settled
1 her stomach. She felt as if she were drowning
1 deep, choppy water with no lifeline in sight.
or she'd fallen in love with this man when she
1dn't even been paying attention. And now he
1s shattering her heart into a million pieces.

"Well, good. That's really good. I'm glad you
o cleared the air."

"Me too."

"So you're packed and ready to leave, I take
?" How her mouth even worked, she wasn't
en certain. She felt as if she could be a pup-
1t, her strings being pulled by an unknown
1tity as she went through the motions.

"Sort of," Drexel answered. Clairey wasn't
1re what that meant and didn't know how to
1 about asking.

Several beats passed in absolute silence. Why in the world was Marnie still smiling? For such a usually perceptive child, she certainly didn't seem to be reading the room correctly.

There was something else about what she was witnessing that didn't sit right. Clairey couldn't quite put her finger on what it could be. She was one big ball of jumbled emotions and bitter disappointment. And tremendous hurt. But there was more to it. Her mind screamed at her that there was something she was missing, something she had to pay attention to. It was important. Something about the scene in front of her didn't compute.

Then she realized what it was. The pile of luggage included three pink and purple Polly Pony bags. Bags that belonged to Marnie. He'd packed for his niece as well as himself.

Her blood turned to ice in her veins. Was he planning on taking Marnie with him? Or leaving Clairey here completely alone? Without either of them and only three kittens to keep her company?

That would certainly explain the girl's giddy mood. But she couldn't even think about what it meant for her. Day after day and night after night sitting here by herself. Alone. With no one around who loved her or cared about her. Once again. A roaring began to sound in her ears, and her vision grew cloudy.

Marnie had walked over to her and was tugging at the hem of her T-shirt. "Uncle Drex has something to ask you."

Clairey did her utmost to smile at the child, but inside a part of her was slowly dying. Clairey had to be strong for her sake. She couldn't risk upsetting Marnie simply because her life was being shattered.

Drexel cleared his throat. "I do, at that. Actually, we both do."

She watched as he seemed to approach her in slow motion. Then he completely confounded her by dropping to one knee in front of them both. He slowly pulled a box out of his front pocket.

Clairey lost the ability to breathe. "Drex," she whispered through lips that had gone desert-dry, "what are you doing?"

"Marnie and I are proposing to you. A real proposal, this time."

Clairey felt her jaw drop. She couldn't have heard him correctly. "You're doing what?"

"Clairey Robi, would you do the honor of marrying me? And Marnie? In a real ceremony with all our friends and loved ones in a dress of your own choosing and a real honeymoon to follow?"

He opened the box to reveal a glittering ring. "You already have the diamond," he explained, a mischievous glint in his eyes. "This

one is glass," he pointed out. "To match you
paired necklaces."

She had to be dreaming this. Clairey was cer
tainly still back in her room. She'd never awak
ened this morning, never crawled out of bed.

None of this was really happening.

"What about the bags? You're all packed t
go to the Middle East."

Drexel made a show of looking around. "Ol
these bags are for all of us. And we're not goin
to the Middle East. Not even close."

"We're not?"

"No. See, there's this wonderful resort on th
Cape that hosts the most extraordinary wec
dings. They even allow pets, believe it or not.
believe you're familiar with it."

"Oh, Drexel."

"It's all been arranged. We just need you t
say yes."

Clairey finally allowed herself to breath
She wasn't being deserted. She was being pro
posed to!

Her heart felt as if it must have swelled t
twice its size in her chest. She pulled Drexel u
to standing and allowed herself to fall into h
arms. His lips found hers in a heady, deep, sou
shattering kiss. A set of skinny arms could b
felt around the tops of her thighs a moment late

She'd been right. This really was a drean

one come true for her. One she never wanted to wake up from.

"Clairey, what's your answer?" Marnie asked in a muffled voice.

Clairey laughed with all the joy and love overflowing in her heart. "Yes!" she declared, looking from Drexel and then down at Marnie's smiling face. "My answer to both of you is absolutely yes!"

EPILOGUE

"I THINK THAT last one was called a sparkler."

Clairey nestled up tighter against her husband, her back to his chest as they watched the stunning fireworks display from the deck of their flybridge boat. The moonlit night was perfect for the stunning show. As was the smooth, calm water of Cape Cod Bay.

"I believe those are Marnie's favorite," she said, reveling in the warmth of his embrace. Her adopted daughter had only left for Colorado three days ago. But Clairey missed her already.

"She seems to be having fun at Bill and Muriel's," Drexel remarked.

"And all those cousins. I think she mentioned about five or six."

Drexel laughed. "At least. Not a bad way for a little girl to spend part of the summer. Running around a ranch with a host of cousins and two doting grandparents."

"And I believe several horses and sheep."

Drexel tightened his arms around Clairey

and nuzzled the top of her head with his chin. "She'll be off to visit Chase and Danielle soon too."

Drexel's brother had come far in the past year. He'd been sober for months and was now even sponsoring others. Drexel was rightly proud of him.

"But she misses Sara," Drexel added. "And her other friends from school."

He'd just given her the perfect segue. Clairey couldn't imagine a better time to tell him the news. She tilted her head and planted a soft kiss on his jaw.

"Speaking of which, I grabbed an application from the Hammond School when I picked her up on the last day. We'll need it soon."

He gently turned her to face him. "An application? Don't tell me we have to renew for Marnie every year. That seems excessive."

She shook her head slowly. "It's not for Marnie. We can't be too early."

He lifted his eyebrows in question. "Not for Marnie. Then, who—?"

Clairey watched with bated breath as his features lit with understanding. His gaze slowly fell to her belly.

"You mean—?"

She couldn't hide her smile. "I don't want to have to try to win another raffle."

She'd barely got the last word out when she

felt herself being lifted off her feet and spun around.

"Are you sure?" he asked when he set her back down.

She nodded. "Confirmed twice. There's no doubt."

He took her lips in his then. Even a year later, it took her breath away every time he kissed her. A year ago, they hadn't even met. Now, the man holding her was the center of her world. And soon they'd be adding yet another source of joy and love to their union.

Clairey couldn't have dreamed she'd ever be so lucky in love. She lifted her face to her husband to tell him exactly that.

Just as another burst of colorful fireworks lit the night sky.

* * * * *

If you enjoyed this story, check out these other great reads from Nina Singh

Her Inconvenient Christmas Reunion
From Tropical Fling to Forever
From Wedding Fling to Baby Surprise
Around the World with the Millionaire

All available now!